And then there was light.

All at once.
Lights.
Colors.
Above the altar.
Around the head of Jesus, his crown of thorns burst into flames of dancing color.

"Sweet Jesus…"

It was Al Culpepper's voice. He stared at the body of Christ as it melted through the spectrum of colors, flickering, casting its rapidly shifting shroud of light over the congregation of nine below. He stared at the face of Christ, only it wasn't the face of Christ he saw painted on the wooden statue, it was his own. He was weeping tears of red, the stigmata, hands, ankles and sides bleeding likewise, tears of blood.

From on high, he grinned at himself and winked, blood smearing the flaking blue paint of his glossy eyes.

Other Titles from DarkTales Publications...

The Asylum Volume 1: The Psycho Ward
Tales of Madness by Doug Clegg and others
Edited by Victor Heck

In Memoriam: Papa, Blake and HPL
Two Stories by Mort Castle

Scary Rednecks and Other Inbred Horrors
Stories by Weston Ochse and David Whitman

DeadTimes
A novel by Yvonne Navarro
(March 2000)

Clickers
A novel by J.F. Gonzalez and Mark Williams
(March 2000)

Eternal Sunset
A novel by Sephera Giron
(April 2000)

Moon On The Water
Stories by Mort Castle
(April 2000)

Secret Life of Colors

by Steve Savile

DarkTales Publications

Kansas City, Missouri • Toledo, Ohio • Chicago, Illinois
2000

Published in the United States by:

Darktales Publications
P.O. Box 675
Grandview, Missouri, 64030

ISBN 0-9672029-4-9

PRINTED IN THE UNITED STATES OF AMERICA
0 1 2 3 4 5 6 7 8 9

To My Marie, The Girl With The Sky In Her Eyes, With Love.

MANHATTAN, where the sun shines red on the upturned faces of angels and antichrists.

If the man coming in out of the rain ever owned a halo, it had long since corroded into flakes of wishes and dead iron. Fat raindrops came down from a charcoal sky as Gabriel Rush let the glass–tinted door swing closed behind him. The gray of cigarette smoke corkscrewed lazily into the haze of stale December air.

Two talkers slumped down beside the cool blue of the fish tank, threadbare elbows steeping in the warm wet circles of beer staining the table between them. Their conversation was muted by the sleazy whisper of saxophone jazz humming in the barroom, drowning their philosophies.

Beneath the stained window of St. Jude, patron of drunks and losers, Nik Lomas stared into his half–empty whiskey glass. Gabriel joined him at the window, waiting for Jake to look up from toweling out a well–worn tumbler. Lomas rolled his glass absently between thick fingers, scratched a line of blue ink across his notepad. His hands were square, with awkward thumbs that jutted out at angles from his forefingers. The skin was hard, ingrained with some chalk–like powder; a journalist born with construction worker's hands.

Gabriel sniffed, wiping a thin trickle of rain from his brow, and lost himself in the glass reflection behind the bar. The face in the mirror had sad eyes, framed by his just–longer–than–shoulder–length, raven–black hair. In the mirror, his eyes were darkened to midnight blue—not the deep blue of the ocean, but close enough that they could have been father and son. There was a small scar beneath the left eye from a cut that couldn't be stitched. *You're no Geronimo*, he told himself, a cynical smile on his lips.

Lomas' voice brought him back. "Jesus, Gabe. You look like shit." Behind the bar, Jake laughed, setting down the well–wiped tumbler. It was a deep grumble that gurgled around inside his ample gut long before it reached his lips. "And you don't smell so good, either. You okay?"

"Depends on what scale we're using," Gabriel answered, rummaging in his pocket for a couple of crumpled bills to put on the counter. "Put it this way: I'm not dead yet, but I'm beginning to think it might not be such a bad idea. Know what I mean?"

Another laugh. "Yeah, only too well, bud. You wanna beer? Course you want a beer, right?" It wasn't a question. Balancing off a thick head of cream, he put the beer on the counter. "You hear about Mike Beijer?"

Gabriel shook his head doubtfully, sketching a childish face in the froth of his drink. "What sort of mouth does he get?" He asked, pointing down with his eyes. "Happy or sad?" The question was part of a ritual carried over from the playground, the bleached yellow faces painted on the concrete beneath the skipping ropes.

"I'm thinking sad. Gabe, Mike took a bite on his .45 last Friday. Pulled the trigger and left half his head on the kitchen wall for his kid to scrape up."

"Jesus…" What little color the rain hadn't stung out of Gabriel's cheeks leeched away as

The vertigo–rush of sound, ghost voices of yesterday launched themselves at him, dancing on the edge of consciousness, the divide between waking and dreaming, the silken hiss of the suicide song howling…to the pulse of light…blinding…white light…the sound of a pan filled with fat and fries hissing on the stove…dark… black…the face of a shocked five year old scrunching balled fists into her eyes, screaming but he can't hear…screaming…screaming…as the greasy back wall runs with thick sugary red water…light…and on the floor…Daddy lies dying…the blood red rose of a bullethole flowering in the side of his head…

the glass shattered in his hand, a jagged splinter biting deep into his palm. The song of suicide haunted him, a lullaby of blood running between his fingers. Gabriel opened his hand, holding it out stupidly while blood and alcohol blended.

"Christ, Gabe. Let me have a look at that."

The splinter had broken off in his palm and looked like an angel's glass tooth in the mouth of his hand.

Hearing the soft brush of the glass doors opening behind him, Gabriel turned on his stool, bleeding hand still held out straight, the drips of red flowering on his Chinos, in time to see a tall, dark–skinned woman glide in. She had a chiseled, bony face, nose a little too long, with ink–stain eyes and the rich black curls of an Afro–American. She looked tired as she placed herself in an empty booth. She moved with the practiced grace of a dancer. Or a hooker, a little voice inside him said.

Two hands on his shoulders turned him around. The bartender had wrapped ice in a towel and was tying it into a makeshift bandage. Gabriel winced at the sting of the cold on the cut. The blood soaked quickly into the wet towel.

On his notepad, Lomas quickly scribbled a note. He ripped off the top sheet and passed it across to Gabriel: *She looks like an angel with her wings on fire.*

His gaze drifted back to the newcomer, the loose cling of her white cotton blouse, the gentle swell of temptation beneath. The red tag of her faded jeans hid a delicacy clothed in cotton. The sweet swell of temptation. Her hair was swept back tightly and braided with black pearls.

"I wouldn't mind getting burned," Gabriel said, crumpling the note in his good hand and slipping it into his pocket. "Who is she?"

Jake laughed his laugh again, not without humor. "Hundred and fifty dollar hooker, my friend. Calls herself Celine, after that singer. Some kind of Hispanic, not that you couldn't guess. Why? Your hormones hearing the call?" His eyebrows creased upwards in a conspiratorial wink as he chuckled to himself.

"Full tom–tom drums and smoke signals. Wait, I'm getting a message...they're saying...one hundred and fifty bucks...one hundred and fifty bucks."

"Go talk to her then, you old silver tongued devil, you. Just don't go making trouble."

"Would I?" Gabriel quipped with a grin.

"I know you, Gabriel."

"That you do, my friend. That you do."

It would have been easy to talk to her, but Gabriel walked back out into the rain of 103rd. Looked at her as she sat framed by the smoky glass of the window of the bar. A sad faced girl alone in a street corner bar, drinking her day away. Between her fingers she twirled a flawed rose. Delicate white petals flaunting their imperfection; a single red tear weeping through the silk weave. There was something desperate in the way her long, sculptured fingernails pinched the fake stem. Her gaze drifted out of the window, to the lamppost across the wide street, some ghost of her past leaning against it, watching her.

Gabriel huddled under the pale shelter of a tenement stoop

and matched her movements, rolling a straggly licorice–paper cigarette between his bloody fingers as he watched her. Lit it. Inhaled. Exhaled jaundiced smoke as a municipal bus rumbled by. His hand ached as he slipped his camera out of his pocket, sneaking a flashless shot of her profile.

Through the lens she looked less an angel, more a melancholy dreamer only anchored to this earth by the weight of her thoughts.

He took four more photographs of her, two of the rose in her hand.

He lay there, legs tangled in the damp bedclothes, staring up at the raindrops as they broke and spilled down the length of the skylight.

They lay in pools of celluloid around the bed; newspaper cut–outs, black–and–whites, Polaroid's. The usual cast of runaways, husbands, and wife–beaters highlighted by the backsplash of light coming off the soft spotlight. There was no glamour in trying to pretend he was Jimmy Stewart. Real life wasn't Rear Window, it was taking candid snaps of melancholy girls in street corner windows. Stealing moments of their souls to put food on the table. Taking photographs of infidelity for the divorce courts. Hustling bucks off paranoia, feeding the green–eyed monster. That was real life. Money, drugs and sex. All shades of the truth, black, white and gray. Gabriel wasn't proud of what he had become, the depths he'd sunk to, the waters so gray they'd drowned the idealist's fire, washed it from his eyes.

His neck was stiff, aching from hours in the rain. Stretching, he scratched at his chest. A black–inked raven was tattooed in the hollow of his breastbone, wing tips touching each of his nipples. The raven, the Black Foot's bird, wisest of all.

"Gabe, we got us a little problem. Can you come in to the Stationhouse?" Mannelli's voice had taken on a distant quality, leaving it half–hidden by the sullen buzz of static. The frail specter of that voice was an ethereal hand from an unwanted past reaching into Gabriel's here and now. An unwanted ghost that dragged his eyes back to the line of photographs on the dresser, each photograph a part of his life he refused to bury: Francesca, another woman with a rose in her hand who had stolen his heart, and Sam, smiling on his third birthday. You'd have been a little over six now, he thought, the sadness of a widower's thoughts sinking like a smooth–sided stone in his stomach.

He pressed his thumbs into his eyes and sniffed back the sleep. 4 a.m. "Yeah, sure. I'm on my way." He fumbled the receiver back into the cradle and sat up.

Next to those, the last photograph, a woman holding cotton candy and smiling mischievously at the camera.

The future.

Gabriel sighed.

The future. In essence, all that meant was someone else to consider.

Ashley.

He found himself thinking about her more and more, her laughter lines and the deep blue–green sea of her eyes. And every time he pictured the lines of her face creasing into that smile of hers he felt a delicious shiver of anticipation wriggle the length of his spine. Somehow, this heightened sensitivity only left him feeling even more distant.

Love?

The morning after the crash all of those photographs spread out across the floor had become his life, the be–all and end–all. A private investigator slugging through the sickness of the streets, the ripped open garbage sacks and the used Coke cans in the gutters of Manhattan and the Bronx. Life reduced to taking photographs of corrupt business partners and wayward spouses. It wasn't a conscious decision, just the way it turned out. He'd even managed to convince himself he liked it that way, up to a point. But that small tingle of anticipation?

Did she love him?

Maybe she couldn't stand him; maybe she just didn't have the heart to tell him as much?

Francesca...Frankie...

Ashley...

Same kettle, very different fish.

Gabriel looked over at the sickly green time as it blurred into four–ten.

"A little problem," he muttered, swinging his legs around and getting out of bed. There was only one type of problem that warranted calling in an ex–homicide detective at 4 a.m., and it wasn't a little one, no matter what Mannelli said.

GABRIEL Rush made the turn into Westwood twenty minutes later.

Despite everything, nothing had changed. *Plus ça change, plus c'est la meme chose*; loosely translated, the more that things change, the more they stay the same. A craggy–faced Chinese woman with snowy locks, baggy black pajamas, and straw sandals shuffled through the mixed smells of ginger, cabbage, onions, and urine. Behind her, her granddaughter laughed, one hand in the pocket of her CK Jeans. A deathless man, his face bleached by years of exhaust fumes and cigarette smoke, leaned against the still dark doorway, the cigarillo hanging limply from his down–turned lips. The wet broom in his hand was matted with Chinese cabbage and onion peelings brushed up from the street. The old man's eyes followed Gabriel as drove slowly by.

Clothing Kit's all–purpose store on the corner of Sedgewick and Columbia was open for the pre–dawn crawl; J.C. Penney's window, a lone black tooth in the smile of the street.

The smells of New York by night still drifted over the neighborhood; not–yet–morning smells all too soon swamped by the dirty smells of the city's dirty life.

The 1956 Black Hawk coughed out a plume of smoke as he pulled in by the fire hydrant in front of The Lotus House, its red–gold hoarding advertising Hunan Szechwan cuisine around the clock. The water dragon roared its discounts and specials. Across the four lanes of traffic the stationhouse loomed, with its rusting fire escapes and carved seven–story facade. Abandoned patrol cars and police bikes lined the curb out front. The old green globes over the door burned dimly, the black legend POLICE faint but clear in the coming light.

Gabriel ducked past the desk sergeant as he entered the building, walked through the empty muster room and went up the stairs; a narrow, winding passage of carved wood, its majestic balustrade old and weak and riddled with woodworm, its metal–tipped steps worn shiny by the shuffling feet of a thousand cops over a hundred years.

The detective squad room could have passed for an office in any insurance company–telephones on desks, computers instead of the Naked Lunch typewriters of a year before. It had been a long time since he'd called this room home...

The door to Mannelli's office concealed a two–way mirror. The detention cage, crammed in a corner, sat all but empty; a wasted looking vagrant huddled up against the back bars, drying out. Steel mesh covered all of the windows. Cardboard wastepaper bins were scattered randomly about the room, the overflowing garbage topped with styrofoam cups, empty Coke cans, pizza boxes and scrunched–up bagel wrappers.

Jack Delgado sat at one of the desks, typing up a rape report with two fingers, his two hundred and ten pounds crammed in behind the Formica, deep–set piggy eyes lost beneath the simian concentration. Another one of New York's finest stood at the bank of cabinets, one hand holding the line to the Assistant DA's office open, the other juggling the contents of a case folder.

Delgado looked up, two fingers hovering. "Fuck me. What're you doing here, Tonto? They kick you off the Reservation for smoking the peace pipe again?"

"Screw you, Kimo–Sabe." Gabriel drew himself a cup of taste-less black treacle from the vending machine, knocked on Mannelli's door and let himself in.

Second–generation Italian, Dan Mannelli was a tall man blessed with a continental swath of dark features and a thick crop of Italian–black hair to match. The lawman had wide shoulders made wider by the padded jacket he'd thrown on—brown leather with the faded painting of an old war girl flaking on the back. He smelled as if he hadn't slept, or washed, in a few days. Dark circles ringed his eyes.

"Stern's just called one in from Lexington," Mannelli said, wast-ing no time on the niceties. "I want your eyes on this one, Gabe. I've got a bad feeling. Some of the stuff sounds...damn it all to freakin' hell...it sounds like he's started pulling some freakin' rit-ual shit...started believing his own freakin' press."

As he downed a mouthful of tepid coffee, Gabriel's eyes drift-ed to the stack of well–thumbed sheets strewn across Mannelli's desk. The coroner's reports on The Trinity's victims one through five; reports six, seven and eight sat neatly stacked on the swivel chair. A New York City street map hung against the back wall. Six red–topped pins with neatly lettered dates etched on their flat heads plotted out the killer's movements over the last three months, each silently marking off the passing of another unfortunate. Another thirty or so pins pooled in the small plastic tray beneath the map, waiting for more spent lives to mark off. A stunted aluminum Christmas tree started and finished Mannelli's concessions to the festive season. Five leaves had browned and curled, burned by a stray cigarette.

"What have you got to go on, Dan? Same MO?"

"That's just it. Killings are usually systematic. You know this shit, Gabe. They have mathematical patterns built into them, stuff for the profilers to build on, be it how they're chosen, killed or dumped afterwards. There's some kind of underlying logic, but not with this guy. He's off on his own personal vendetta that just happens to involve carving elaborate patterns all over his victims 'bodies."

ONE of the two patrolmen standing in front of 1143 Lexington flagged them down as they approached.

Closing the Black Hawk's door behind him, Mannelli called to the uniform: "Where's Stern?"

"Up on the third, Lieutenant," the officer answered, falling back into position beside his partner as they went through the open door.

The door to the third floor studio stood open; letting the bad air circulate. Gabriel breathed deeply, as if trying to smell any traces the murderer might have left behind; the stench of his rotten soul clinging to the grease and the fat in the frying pans. The floor was covered by cracked linoleum, the checkerboard pattern broken up by missing tiles and the gap–toothed grin of the floorboards beneath. A grubby kitchenette stacked with rotten food and the chitinous sound of hatching maggots ran the length of the room. A bed sat next to an open window, its fittings tarnished brass, and a chipboard chest of drawers. Not many possessions to mark the passing of a life.

Inside the room, Gabriel's guess about the bad air confirmed itself.

The body of a white man, naked but for a pair of black stockings, suspenders and patent leather heels, stretched flat on his back, lay on the sagging mattress. His pallid face was set at right angles to his shoulders; his sightless, half–eaten eyes still open on death. The blood had drained away to his legs, leaving a stark blue discoloration around his lower belly. An elaborate series of cuts in the dead flesh made the body and arms of a crucifix. Suspended from each arm, the cups of a scale, weighing out sins and atonement. A single large cut opened him from balls to throat, splitting the image neatly in two.

The neck of a broken wine bottle lay on the floor, clotted blood clinging to its jagged edges.

The dead man's face was all he needed to see the final mercy death had been when it finally claimed him; set as it was in a cruel sculpture of agony forever recorded by the hand of rigor mortis.

Bill Stern, Costello to Mannelli's Abbott, was standing over the body, a thick Cuban cigar jutting out of the corner of his dour mouth. Stern's face was deeply seamed and pitted with the crags and craters of acne from twenty–five years ago. "Good to see ya, Gabe. Danny. Not a pretty picture is it?" He grumbled, every other word punctuated by a wispy puffball of smoke.

Gabriel moved over to the window and stared out at the stark stretch of the Manhattan skyline. The rain might have stopped for the morning, but the sky over the city was slashed with streaks of silver, gray and white; the sky a backdrop to a latticework of cold, rippling clouds and the fading outline of a werewolf moon.

Using the hard edge of a fingernail, Gabriel traced the outline of two simplistic shapes carved into the wooden sill. A tadpole and a crude frog. Old magic...the metamorphosis from water to earth...he shook his head, thinking of his father's tales of the Old Man who defeated the terrible underwater enemies of mankind. The perpetual war between the sky and the water spirits. Salt had been powdered into the opened grains of the wood. Next to white man wardings...this was one scared man.

He scratched the tattooed relic on his chest, looking for inspiration.

Great Spirit, help me, he thought bitterly, and said, "Hey Dan, something over here you ought to see."

Forensics took photos of the warding from above and from either side while he explained its significance. The clash of cultures and superstitions. Stern grunted, making notes in his pad, then thumbed over a page and scrawled: SALVATION DAMNATION TRINITY. The gospel according to Bill Stern. "Wait 'til you get a load of this, though. Shirley Bassey here's the priest from St. Malachy's. Don't seem to me like a man of God would be messin' with your Voodoo, Gabe. No matter how scared he was."

Gabriel's fingers strayed back to his chest, seeking the comfort of the raven. He didn't argue, simply slipped the camera from his pocket and took three quick shots of the crime scene. He knew the superstitions and the hexes as well as he knew the scent of rain. You can take the man out of the Reservation, but you can't take the Indian from his soul, and that was the bitterest irony because that was exactly what he'd done, playing along with their dirty White Man magic, sacrificing the Great Spirit to the four winds. My world has moved on, he told himself, knowing it sounded like the lame excuse it was. There's no place for the old ways in my life, no place...his fingers scratched almost angrily at the tattoo, denying the lie of his thoughts.

"You sure about that, Bill?"

"Yeah, had a run in with him three years back. Same night Al Culpepper was shot. The padre here gave last rites after...After that doped–up speedfreak put a slug through his head. Killed in a fuckin' church...Killed in the fuckin' arms of God..." Stern sucked on his cigar, let out a shaky breath.

Gabriel moved over to the body, laying his hand palm flat on the clammy skin. His fingers stopped moving as they touched the ugly Trinity tattoo, his thoughts blind men suddenly cursed with the gift of sight. Touching the dead man was like feeling the fangs of an electric serpent sinking into his fingertips, the venomous contact burning up through his arm, the violently discharged voltage sending him reeling as

The boy rose from his knees, looking bewildered, blank...his Latino lips moved, suddenly hungry to taste the fresh air...he was circled by the black–eyed gaze of guns...the smoke curling from the votive candles, a lazy lover done dying for them...and then the silent screams and the not–so–silent curses as the boy's body was suddenly forced into a twisting, jerking dance by their bullets...spinning, arms drowning and dying as his body crashed into the stone altar...up above, the crucifix...wearing its crown of thorns...drifting down, breathing its sickness into the boy...and the boy rising again...reaching out to touch his cheek, a fingernail burning its scar into his face while the stained window wept its tears of broken glass...

the lightbulb hanging from the bare flex shattered, raining hot glass on his scalp and the dead padre's rumpled sheets. Gabriel recoiled involuntarily, hands flying up, crushing the heels of his palms against his temples, face twisting in a mask of agony.

"Get...out...of...my...head..." The words hissed between clenched teeth even as he started to collapse. His legs buckled and he hit the floor, head clipping off the side of the bed with a sickening crunch.

Mannelli reacted first, making a grab for thin air as Gabriel slipped through his fingers. His face a mask of concern, he knelt down beside Rush. "You okay, Gabe?" He reached out, touched his forehead.

Gabriel's eyelids fluttered, reacting to the sounds, the intrusion of light, bringing him back. His fingers touched the gash left by the edge of the bed, tentatively feeling out the wound. The scar on his left cheek throbbed. Sickness knifed his stomach, but that was all. It came and it went. He blew out a pained breath. A ragged sigh. "I'm not feeling so good, this whole place is spinning..." He bit back the urge to tell Mannelli, to explain, how his world was turning itself upside down.

Mannelli helped him to his feet, supported him. "You've got to lay off the Peace Pipe," his friend joked, the hardened cop again, trying to make light of Gabriel's sudden collapse. "I suppose it's too much to ask, but I don't suppose there were any witnesses, were there Bill?"

"The old lady downstairs reported it. Found him like this when she came up to give him his early morning wake–up call. Seems she used to get the padre up at four every morning so he could go down in time to deliver the morning Mass."

"Now there's devotion for you—four every morning, huh?"

"Yep. Anyways, the doc's in with her right now, treating her for shock. Poor old cow's gonna be on Prozac 'til she croaks, but as far as I can tell, she didn't see shit."

"Sure is getting to be repetitive, ain't it?"

"You think?"

"How long's he been like this?" Mannelli nodded downwards, eyes straying back to the gray putty beneath the suspenders.

"About eighteen hours, give or take. We'll have to wait for the Morgue to give us anything more precise. If it's another one of The Trinity's and not some other freak out for a good time, this takes him on to four hookers, two cops, a college kid, a city girl and a transvestite preacher. Can't make up my mind if he is moving up or down in the world."

"Too fucking funny, Bill. Cover the padre up, will ya?"

"WHO are you?" Gabriel wondered softly. The red–tinged Judas light of the dark room bled across the drying prints, coloring his thoughts.

Looking down at the girl in the developing tray, he drew on the unfiltered nicotine of his roll–up. A wisp of smoke coiled around her, lingering, like the languid arms of a lazy lover. He felt a long way from the usual cast of runaways and wife–beaters, lost in a rabbit–warren of dirty streets and dirtier lives.

Carefully, he used a pair of plastic tweezers to res-cue the contact sheet from the shallow tray of devel-oping fluid, ran it through a pan of fixative and then a wash before hanging it from the roped–up washing line. He felt cold looking at her like this, reduced to the size of a thumbnail gazing through five of the ten squares. The definition wasn't particularly sharp in any of them, but it was recognizably her.

As Gabriel ran his eyes over the contacts, one stood out. One where her sad eyes were aware, looked out through the wet paper and saw deep into his own.

Turning his back on her, he turned off the overhead red and went through to the luncheonette to grab a Pepsi from the cool-er. It was a serious case of Old Mother Hubbard syndrome in there. A pita bread growing its own penicillin cultures, half a green bell pepper and a clutch of carrots—otherwise, the cup-board was bare.

Gabriel popped the can's tab. His neck was stiff, ached from hours in the rain and not enough sleep.

In the bathroom, he set the shower running, opened the cabi-net and rescued a half–popped foil of Tylenol, swallowed, stripped and stepped in, savoring the delicious sting of the water on his skin, tiny burns that ran like scalpel blades down the length of his back. Gabriel planted his hands against the wall tiles and simply soaked, thinking about sleep, thinking about the girl with the flower, thinking about the transvestite preacher's labyrinth of bloody tattoos. Thinking about the boy who wouldn't die, even in his dreams...

As an insipid sun rose over Manhattan, sending its pale golden shafts into the bedroom, Gabriel Rush tossed and turned fitfully, sleep taunting him with its infinite possibilities and unanswered prayers. The sun that hid the one unchangeable thing in his world, the stars, the sky river and the giant turtle. The same stars that had looked down on the First Father and old Saukamappee's thunderbirds.

His dream–self was standing on a high place, looking down over a city of colored glass, being buffeted and battered by a howling wind. Ice chapped against his fingers, freezing into a brittle jigsaw of crystals that cracked and flaked away, stealing skin.

He wasn't alone.

Daniel Mannelli was with him; though not the Mannelli he knew, his companion was Mannelli just the same. That dream identity where the soul clad itself with whatever skin it desired. Together, they stood side by side, gazing down onto a crystal–coated sheet of ice, watching as ribbons of colored gossamer thread cavorted through the streets of the glacial wasteland.

All around him, things were wrong.

There was something...

Not quite a face.

Something else...a crown...of glass thorns...

Spectral, ethereal, moving through the sunlight.

"I'm walking in your footsteps, Indian," the voice of the nightmare rasped. "I'm the end of your everything...I will..." It paused for a full second, letting the nightmare's wind sing its lonely lament. When the voice came back to him it was filled with venomous hatred. "Taste your soul..."

The image shattered, and he fell, plunged, down and down into the arms of a gnarled tree of clear glass...

The echo of a word carried back to him as he woke.

"Soon..."

HE woke feeling worse for the few hours of restless sleep.

There was an overexposed fuzz over part of her face in one of the photographs. Nothing precise, but something peculiar. It could have been dirt on the lens or from the window, there had been enough glass between them, but then the smear would have been on all of the shots.

He took the contact sheet down from the washing line and used a fisheye lens to magnify the girl.

Her long lashes, thick with mascara, guarded her eyes. He saw it then, the substance in the haze, the body and form of the illusion, melting into her left cheek, the mark of the Trinity; Father, Son and Holy Ghost, the simple rendition of three from one carved into her cheek...

A body with a fetus carved where a stomach should be, the pair surrounded by a bloody nimbus that was mark of the ghost...

Quickly, Gabriel checked the single shot of the dead preacher. There was something on the dead man's cheek, amid the swirl of cuts, but it was too still too small to be certain.

It could be anything, he told himself but even as he thought the thought, he knew exactly what he'd find there if he made an enlargement:

The mark of The Trinity.

GABRIEL developed the reflections of two souls in the dark room. A4 exposures of the window girl and the dead preacher. He half–hoped (but didn't expect) that the strange tattoo–haze over her cheek would be proved benign; a smudge or smear on the glass between them, and not the Trinity tattoo at all.

He slipped them into a manila envelope along with photographs of The Trinity killer's other victims. The quality of the printouts was grainy, but each one shared the same macabre tattoo on left cheek.

Gabriel went back to the bar on Bourbon Street because he didn't know where else to go. Stood across the street, camera in hand. Waited for her. Counted the buses going one way in the rush hour traffic and the yellow cabs coming the other. Felt the subway train rumble by beneath the sidewalk and lost count. Watched a red faced Santa Claus rifling the bins for scraps, the neck of a brown baggie–wrapped bottle peering out of a festive pocket.

Someone else was in her seat, holding a copy of *The New York Times* at a distance to keep the print in focus. Gabriel stole a single shot of the reading man, more to dismiss the doubt that by rights should have been niggling at the back of his mind. After that, he went inside and settled into a comfortable lean against the bar, a slowly settling Guinness and a saucer full of cashew nuts to chew the wait out.

The barroom was mothballed in the cheap gasoline scent that was so essentially New York City.

She came in at lunchtime, just after, ordered an iced lemon tea and nothing else. As she had the day before, the sad–faced girl who called herself Celine sat at her window table and stared out at the lamppost across the street, looking for her savior on the wet sidewalk.

Gabriel slipped the camera out of his pocket and stole a single flashless snap of her profile, left side, before he put it away again; this one for confirmation of the impossible. Ran a hand through his hair and walked across to where she sat, squeezed into the booth opposite her and put his hands flat on the table between them. "Can we talk? Someplace private?"

Without looking up, she said, "The booth's occupied, mister."

Her voice was low, rich, like the tremble of the black keys on a piano; and her smell...

...Sweetness; of expensive cologne, rose shampoo and scented bubble bath. Delicate scents fresh from the perfume counter in Bloomingdale's.

"You're Celine, right? Humor me, Celine." He took a roll of bills from the pocket of his Chinos, rifled them and pulled out three fifty's. Sliding them across the table, Gabriel stopped an inch short of her long, sculptured fingernails. They were plastic, fake, he noticed, seeing a leaking glue–bubble. "I just want to talk, even if I have to pay the going rate."

"For Christ's sake," she breathed, her accent a slow southern drawl, and fixed him with a long suffering look with about as much warmth in it as a dead caveman frozen in an ice floe. "It ain't even three–thirty in the afternoon, and I ain't working this place, no way, no how. So put your fucking money away."

"Hey, hey. Sorry. Look, this has started all wrong. I'm not look-ing for a date. I need to talk to you." Gabriel held out his hands, palms pressed out in a gesture of peace, one bandaged, one bare, shrugged his thickset shoulders. *What am I supposed to say? I used to be a cop until I killed my own son...*

She looked at him, her ink–stain eyes moving down the lines of his chest, to the lip of the table and back in open appraisal to his face, saw the pain his eyes and misunderstood. "Talk all you like," she said. "I ain't promising I'll listen."

He could feel the dusky bristlings of three–thirty shadow pok-ing through his olive tanned chin. There was no nice way to say what he had to say, so he slid a photograph from the envelope and slid it across the table. "Look at the picture, tell me what you see."

Celine studied the photo in careful silence. Then said: "A shad-ow, something. On my cheek. When did you take these?"

"Yesterday...I saw you sitting here, thought it was a good pic-ture. I've got some other photos. They're pretty ugly but I want you to look at them, same deal. Tell me what you see, okay?" He put the envelope on the table, let her do it in her own time. Let her make up her own mind.

One by one Celine withdrew the brutal images, laying them out in a macabre fan; the dead faces; the injuries; the Trinity, father, son and bloody ghost carved into each cheek in turn. She looked back at her own photograph. Back at the ghost there, superimposed on her face, looking for the trickery but not finding it. Silence, stunned. Then:

"You think I'm part of this? That I'm going to get hurt? Is that it?"

"Like I said, humor me." There was just the merest hint of irony in Gabriel's voice. He'd come so close to saying trust me, and that would have been a mistake, given the circumstances. This girl's world was being turned upside down by a stranger, asking for her trust while he did it was too much, too soon. Instead he asked: "Have you got friends you can stay with for a couple of days? Somewhere to go?" Safe ground. "Surround yourself by familiar faces, maybe take a few days off from meeting strangers. Give this some time to blow over. It's probably nothing but...just humor me, okay?"

She nodded mutely, staring at the mess of the padre's body.

He left the number of his mobile, the number back at the apartment, Mannelli's number at the Westwood Precinct, and the photographs for her to think about.

HE wondered, quietly, as he looked out at the banks of sleazy neon that advertised the peepshow across the way, what they would have thought of their precious God driving around in a blood–red, stolen Pontiac Bonneville with golden licks of flame scorched along its door panels and a horn that whistled Dixie.

It was loud, and crude, and of course unnecessary, but they were giving him so much to live up to, so many standards to meet, that he had to at least make the effort.

Not that spending between ten and twelve hours a night living inside a cramped '87 Bonneville was a good deal, or worth even half the pain. She guzzled juice like a bar–propping lush chasing away the blues on a bad day, reeked with the attar of octane and oil and lived her life among the red–lined sectors of the gauges.

He was stiff, sore, aches and pains nagging away around the base of his spine and along the length of his shoulders.

Irritating little nothings.

It was all a case of patience and picking the moment.

He smiled into the rear–view mirror. This was his moment. Written in the stars.

Gunning the engine, he moved on, the Pontiac crawling along the length of the curb like a grubbing snail, and turned a corner. This part of the city seemed to be filled with boarded–up shops and abandoned lots, as if the lifeblood of the entire neighborhood had been drained away and its corpse left out to rot under the glare of the bitter moon.

The idea had a certain something.

The sheets of plywood boarding up the shop fronts were covered with stickers for touring rock bands, sprayed over with colorful layers of inventive graffiti.

The Unfortunate stood alone, her eyes stains of ink on her midnight face. Behind her, an oversized banner was plastered across the window of an out–of–fashion carpet warehouse. This grubby little back alley, with its festering garbage and forgotten shops, could have been a sliproad onto Interstate 101, a road to nowhere.

Puddles of dull lamplight mottled the damp flagstones, highlighting the tumbling food wrappers and sheets of yesterday's news, where unbroken streetlights still cast their own shine, creating darkness within the mouths of doorways and blackness around corners. The lights were few and very far between.

The Unfortunate shifted her gaze away from the Middle Distance as the dipped headlights of the Pontiac rolled gradually closer.

Coming level, he reached across and rolled the window down halfway, stubbing the wet–lipped dog–end of his cigarette out in the flip–front ashtray. The Unfortunate stooped and peered in through the tight opening, her eyes alert and on guard.

A wry little smile played on his lips as he put on his face for her.

Close up, the Unfortunate was nothing more than a sad–faced young girl masquerading as a dark–skinned honey with her hair braided into strings of black pearls and lipstick–smudged lips the vivid red of sex. It didn't matter, an artist had carved her face with a delicate chisel, working miracles that make–up couldn't hide.

"You looking for another date, sweetie?" she asked, parting those lipstick–smeared lips to tease her tongue slowly along the gloss. "I've kept that rose you gave me last time."

Reaching across to the glove compartment he lifted out a handful of dog–eared dollar bills, the faces of dead presidents crumpling in his hand. "Thought we could go for a ride," he answered.

"So, where're we going?" she laughed, moving around the hood towards the passenger door and climbing in.

"Straight to heaven, I think…" His smile spread into the toothy rictus of a door–to–door salesman closing in for the kill, lips splitting his face neater than the edge of any knife could.

He touched the soft curve of her left cheek, tracing the outline of a picture that had been waiting for the canvas of her body before it could be drawn.

ten

UNDER direction, he drove the Unfortunate back to the apartment she rented out on the fifteenth floor of a crumbling high–rise that towered over the banks of the Hudson. Riding up in the elevator she had told him to call her Celine, like the singer. Laughing as the doors opened on her floor, she had said she felt happier being a Celine, like she was a different person. It was a way of hiding from reality that suited her just fine.

He stopped listening to her constant prattle as she struggled with the lock and deadbolt, almost pushed passed her in his hurry to get inside. Didn't stop walking until his fingers were tapping on the windowsill, scratching the fake wood.

He could see out onto the Hudson, a strip of Riverside, down to the Soldier's and Sailor's Monument, and along, to the skeletal span of the George Washington Bridge lit up in the misty distance. Naked girders and stacked up slabs of concrete surrounded the body of another half–made building. It looked like an exposed ribcage. All bones and wounds too deep and too wide for it to live. Life in negative. Where life was being poured into it, it looked as if the towering skyscraper was caving in and dying on its shaky feet.

Celine didn't join him at the window.

He hadn't heard her stop talking, but when he turned he saw her fingers slip the shoulder of her blouse back on the feverish flesh of her shoulder, the fabric rustling like the silken rush of snow as it fell to the floor. She smiled at him, unsure. His eyes drifted over the black lace, lingering on her belly as if it were the most erotic treasure she had to offer. She stepped out of her jeans. The light danced across the gentle swell of her hip, half–gleaming; the skin beneath freshly waxed with some kind of body oil. Tangles of black curled onto her thigh, too long and too thick to be attractive.

"You should shave," he said.

"Ain't no refund, pal," Celine replied, turning on the CD. John Popper's harmonica cut the cooling air and she began to dance, a kind of shiver that seemed to squirm the length of her body in a teasingly painful performance. From toes to waist, hips to head and back down again.

"Now," she said, hands resting on the mocha flesh of her thighs, massaging just a few inches from those tight black curls. "Are you gonna fuck me or not?"

"Come here and unbuckle me," was his answer, that smile sneaking back. The kill so close... "It'd be a crime to waste that lip gloss, sugar."

She laughed her laugh and there was no innocence in that bell as she went down on her knees, fingers dragging over the teeth of his zipper before they tugged at the belt. Fingers curled around him, brought him to her lips.

He forced her to take him in too deeply, pressed as he looked down at the top of her head, then at her eyes as she looked up at him, that desperate need to please in her ink–stain eyes.

He let her make him come, kept his hands braced on the back of her head while he skull–fucked her until his semen was dribbling out of the corners of her wet mouth.

"Nice. But not worth a hundred and fifty bucks," he said, putting himself away. "I need a drink and ten minutes so I can get my money's worth. Where'd you keep the liquor?"

"Through there," she said, wiping the back of her hand across her mouth, cleaning up his mess.

He left her on her knees and went through to the kitchen. In a second he had found what he was looking for, the plastic wrap; it sat on a wooden chopping board beside the skillet. Quietly, so as not to be heard, he tore off a strip long enough for what he had in mind and walked back into the lounge.

Celine was still on her knees, her hand still raised to her lips as if his semen had somehow burned her and she was feeling the blisters left behind.

He walked up behind her, "You should call yourself Felitia," he said and laughed at his own joke. As her head started to turn his laugh turned into the harsh bray of a mule. He snatched up a fistful of her hair and jerked her backwards onto her back, not caring that she screamed against the unnatural angle he forced her legs into before he kicked them out from under her. He slapped her across the face.

Before Celine could start to get up, he dropped onto her heaving chest. The breath leaked out of her like a balloon going down. He punched her in the throat. Hard. Her eyes bugged and those chiseled layers of flesh reddened as she gagged, gasping for air that wasn't there.

In his hand the plastic wrap had folded on itself, wrinkling up.

Celine squirmed, wriggling her body about like a lizard trapped in a sardine tin, but his knees kept her arms pinned and his weight held her chest.

Taking his time, he peeled the plastic wrap away from itself, opening the sheet out again, and doubling its thickness so she couldn't somehow suck a breath through it, he stretched it taut across Celine's mouth and nose.

Her flattened lips paled as her body bucked and thrashed about wildly under him but he rode her until there was nothing left, Celine's face cold and dead against his groin, where the whole erotic dance had started.

Standing again, he peeled away the plastic wrap and took out his knife, began cutting, cutting, cutting...carved the shape of a tree into her belly, opened her up lips to lips and unraveled her, laying the gray coils of intestine out like so many umbilical cords looping back to the tree of life...carved the image of a pregnant man on her left cheek, smeared the blood into a halo...The Father, Son and Holy Ghost...

Finally, he dipped his hands inside her, sank himself into the bottom of Celine, feeling out every inch of her insides, brought his bloody hands back up to his lips, hands pulsing with an incandescent light that was everything vile in the world, and tasted her sweet, secret flesh the way God had meant him to.

CLEAN, he walked back out into the city, past the Pontiac and away, whistling softly to himself as he went...All Along The Watchtower...

Thin gossamer threads of vapor, like finely crafted webs of spider's silk, licked at the worn down heals of his neubuck boots, something like ice cracking on the sidewalk in his wake.

A fallen angel of no particular age, like so many other fallen souls in the twilight city; dressed in faded Levi's and an off-white shirt; very much alive to the many possibilities of the long night.

Just another one of the crowd.

THAT dream again, the almost–face and the battering winds.

This time Gabriel tried to recapture it in pen and ink after he woke. An impossibly tall monolith. He wasn't brilliant, but he was good. Every unsteady, inked line caught and reflected another aspect of the serpentine twists and frenzied architecture of his dream tower, laying down a mass of sky–catching reflections amid the elongated walls of plated glass as they stretched higher, toward the circlet of marsh-mallow cloud hidden beyond the beckoning edge of the paper.

The drawing took most of the morning, and it was made more difficult by the pain in his hand whenev-er a careless movement stretched the healing wound. Bob Dylan told him he made love just like a woman, which put a smile on his face while he drew.

Still smiling, Gabriel added a crudely drawn stick man at the top of the tower, unconsciously changing pens to ink in a red out-line.

Marooned amid the bleak whiteness of the paper, set safely on the tower of reflections, the stick man twisted its head as if to look up at its creator.

It's still part of the dream, Gabriel told himself, the ache in his hand denying him even that small comfort. *The part that should have died when the sunlight touched my eyes. That's all it is, a part of the dream...*

Gabriel dropped the pen. Dylan stopped singing. The feature-less face pressed against the barrier of paper, a writhing jumble of red lines struggling to breach the containing weave. For a second, between songs, he was faced with the irrational fear that the paper would split open and the thing from his dream would reach through to seize him by the throat with greasy, scaled claws...

Through the pregnant swell of the paper–face Gabriel saw the repulsive mambo of squirming maggots, their bodies splashed with the semi–gloss sheen of red. Slick with blood. The face began to pulse in time with the thunderous heartbeat booming against his eardrums.

Even as he stared, the weave of the paper began to slowly unknit: thin, fibrous strands of woven pulp peeling back on themselves rather than going up against the press of the nightmarish paper–face. Radiated light, red, like the leprous paste of blood, squeezed through the tiny cracks as, heartbeat by heartbeat, the face began to unknit itself.

Great Spirit, First Father, help me, "Go! Go! Back to the dream," he hissed, fingers pressing painfully into his temples as his eyes screwed up refusing to see.

The eyes of the paper–face went wide, a fissure cracking its cheek like the track of a shed tear, re–knit, and the stick man's colored body started on a final, deadly plummet, arms wind-milling wildly as it plunged out of the cartoon sky...

Without looking back, Gabriel turned away, leaving his draw-ing to die its unnatural death.

He arrived at the Westwood Precinct an hour before the preliminary on The Trinity Killer's Number Nine. Father Joseph D'Angelo was due through from downtown. Didn't talk about the dreams or the stick man's suicide plunge.

Mannelli swallowed a mouthful of tepid coffee and put down the styrofoam cup, a warm wet circle ringing the after–face of Maria Massey, the hooker with a heart of gold. Number One. Where the before–face was pretty, not stunning but enough to bring the eye back for a second look, the after–face was a mess of bloody carvings washed clean and cut deep. It was easy to see patches where the ruined skin had started to swell, which made Mannelli think she had still been alive when the cutting began.

According to the reports, four of The Trinity's eight confirmed victims—Caroline Öberg, Jessica McMahon, Lindy Matther and Anna Selvin—showed, not the bruising of abuse, but simply signs of sexual activity...as well as mild hemorrhaging and low T– and white cell–counts, cognizant as the first pernicious touch of the HIV virus.

Mannelli pulled a clean sheet of A4 from a large legal pad and wrote himself a summary of all the murders to date, with basic details for each killing and a few sketchy suppositions of his own. Where the bodies were discovered, by whom, injuries, clothing. The idea of a Gay Plague killer was there. Beside it was a ringed picture of the pregnant man which they had all assumed was part of the Holy Trinity.

The four HIV girls backed up the theory as far as the two cops, Seth Lawson and Ben Sheldon, but then the idea died—a response to a reported breaking and entering above a 7–Eleven in East Tremont.

Four prostitutes, two cops, a college boy, a city woman and a partridge in a pear tree...

Barring victims, times and dates, he was left with eight seemingly unrelated murders.

Some of the killings involved sexual assault, but not all of them. Four, the HIV virus was eating away at the corpse. One involved robbery gone haywire. Two, drugs. In some cases the victims' bodies showed evidence to suggest extreme tortures undergone before death, in others they were almost untouched. Almost.

Only two facts remained anchored amid a sea of floating variables; the cause of death in each case, despite the variety of wounds: asphyxiation. The trademark: the trinity tattoo on the left cheek, Father, Son and Holy Ghost.

No matter what other cruel and unusual punishments had been metered out, mutilation, slashing, dismemberment—these two constants proved that the same man had perpetrated each of the seemingly random killings.

Precious little, and nothing they didn't already know.

There were no fingerprints to go on, but in three cases there was semen. Caroline Öberg's body had yielded three different traces; Lindy Matther's two, both recent; and Anne Selvin's, four, one a match with Caroline Öberg. The matching samples had been recovered from the girl's throat in both cases.

His handwriting covered three pages by the time he'd finished transcribing everything he knew about The Trinity Killer's modus operandi. There were too many question marks and blind alleys where things that should have simply didn't link. They were missing something...

Mannelli had pretty much given up hope that they would find it. It wasn't going to be that simple.

He walked over to the window and braced his hands against the wooden windowsill, fingers skirting the peeling emulsion as he looked out from his ivory asylum onto the city below. His breath frosted on the pane of glass.

The window reflected his worn face; the dark puffs under his reddened eyes and the gloomy, growing crack between his neck and shirt collar.

Behind him, Gabriel looked at the reflection, seeing the face of a friend slowly decaying into a pale shade of itself, a good man's soul being sucked dry, and shivered. His own photograph of Celine lay on top of the coroner's report for Seth Lawson, the ghost of that damned tattoo taunting their helplessness.

On the other side of the closed door, with the faint background chorus of Christmas carols, Jack Delgado fielded another crank call. His in–tray held fifty–six memos, each headed up 'Trinity Killer', each one a phoned–in confession from someone desperate to get their sins off their chests. Next to the confessions he had a pile of 'Could–Be's' and psychiatric evaluations, two hundred thick; the results of concerned neighbors, wives, girl-friends, employers, and friends eager to account for the where-abouts of loved ones, friends and subordinates. The simple process of feeding the useless facts into the database would take days, and there were no guarantees that the precious model winging its way down from Quantico would be any more use than a fart in a wet hole. More spurious facts were coming in by the hour.

Mannelli turned away from the window, leaving his half–cup of cold coffee behind as he walked back to the desk. Face up was the preliminary case report on Rebecca Scott, Number Six. Two red words, 'Trinity Homicide' were scrawled in Jack Delgado's handwriting across the manila cover.

He knew the Scott girl's case by heart: death by asphyxiation; mild contusions on the cerebral cortex, consistent with a rain of heavy blows to the head, mating with the forensics report on the iron firepoker found at the scene; a ruptured spleen; wounds carved to a depth of 5 millimeters depicting a gravid male body surrounded by more cuts that might have been some kind of aura; universal bruising and lesions around the base of the spine and lower torso; series of shallow, cosmetic scratches around the vaginal entrance; and mild hemorrhaging, probably the result of excessive shock.

He knew all of the open case files, and could take an educat-ed guess at the one coming in.

But something just didn't fit.

It wasn't coming together in any sort of recognizable pattern he'd seen before.

"Ritual killings," he said aloud, and shook his head.

"My father used to say that if you stare too long at something you stop seeing the truth of it. For all his failings, there is some truth in that, Dan."

Grunting, Mannelli shifted the weight of reports off his chair and sat himself down behind the desk to read through them again, as if by staring at the words for long enough an answer would begin the slow meandering dance from the paper and into his eyes.

BILL Stern watched the pathologist's careless artistry, fascinated and simultaneously sickened by the way the man's hands moved through the cold stew of organ and sinew inside the nine–inch slash that cut through Father Joseph D'Angelo's slight pot–belly, pulling and probing with all the consummate skills of a fish–gutter.

"I think I preferred looking at him in stockings," he said. "What's it they say, Doc? We're all the same color inside?"

"Mmmm…" Ellery mused, tutting as something else failed to add up to his professional expectation.

"Notice how they never say we look like a cold bowl of Hungarian goulash?"

Flecks of the dead padre's blood slicked off Ellery's surgical gloves, splashing a film of thin crimson over the kidney tray on the trolley, as he swapped the thick–bladed scalpel he had been probing with for a more precisely edged blade.

"So, what do you reckon, Doc?"

"Hard to say," the pathologist hedged, slicing through another rasher of fatty tissue to expose the motorway of abandoned veins. "For sure. It certainly looks like he died before the first of the knife wounds was inflicted, see here?" he said, pointing at the rough circle of severed veins and arteries with the scarlet–tainted tip of the scalpel. "Not much evidence of bleeding. If the wounds are fresh this would suggest a cardio–vascular failure. In fact, I think I would go so far as to suggest that this major wound, here," he ran the scalpel blade the length of the cut from the dead padre's groin to his neck, "was inflicted somewhere in the region of ten to fifteen hours after the time of death. However, the obvious lack of muscle deterioration would rule out the likelihood of any greater length of time."

The pathologist prodded at the fatty tissue of the stomach wall. "The muscle still hasn't tightened too badly. Yet, that said, there are signs of several bunched clusters of corded sinew to go against it being much less than ten hours, give or take the effects of cold and that sort of thing." Ellery paused, scratching at his bearded cheek.

"So what you're saying is it wasn't the knife that killed him? Right?"

"I'd have to say no. Asphyxiation. The damage to his thorax is extreme, distending of the atlas and axis, and discoloration of internal tissue suggests some sort of struggle. Look at the slight bruising around his mouth and nose. Most probably from the attacker's knuckles pressing down against the face while he struggled."

"Number Nine, then?" Stern asked, although he already knew the answer.

"Almost certainly," Ellery conceded, dropping his scalpel into the kidney tray. "Even without the Trinity tattoo on the left cheek I'd be given to believe that this was our man again."

"Shit."

"That's about the size of it," Ellery agreed. "Look, you don't have to stop around while I sew him up. It'll only take a few minutes. Why don't you go through to reception and grab a coffee. I'll come through when I've finished up and we can go grab something stronger. This kind of thing always makes me want a drink, just to get the taste of death out of my mouth."

"Just point me in the direction of the kettle, Doc. I'll take care of the rest."

THE telephone rang.

Once. Twice. Three times.

Mannelli didn't move, so Gabriel answered it. He listened for a moment, then said, "Right," and hung up. Holding a half–eaten bagel, he walked across to the street map, took out a flat–topped pin and marked off a spot over on Lexington, near the Lincoln Tunnel.

The padre's cramped apartment.

"D'Angelo's one of his," he said without looking around. "Number Nine."

Two more calls came in within the hour.

The first from a distraught Port Authority Official who had had the misfortune to find his secretary stripped naked and laid out across his desk with a steel bar buried fist deep in her anus. The second, from a man who had tried to get into his neighbor's apartment. He'd knocked twice more, then opened the mailbox and noticed the smell.

An hour later, as Dan Mannelli faced down a barrage of leading questions from the pariahs of the press and Bill Stern picked up the phone to answer a call from Brendon Ellery, Jack Delgado parked behind an abandoned Pontiac Bonneville on the Riverside, breathed deeply on the Hudson's nearly fresh Christmas air, and walked in on The Trinity's tenth victim.

THE camera focused on a new face in the crowd. A woman, tall, striking with stark winter–gray eyes, the sharp rise of a carved nose and the square curves of a stubborn jaw, all white against the backdrop of straight black hair. A few other familiar faces mixed in with the pack of piranhas. Lomas scribbling something in his pad.

"Well, that is comforting to know, Lieutenant Mannelli. Tell me, out of interest, how long do you plan to wait this thing out? A day, two? People are busy dying, Lieutenant. How many more people have to die before you find this Monster?"

Her eyes met his, locked, unwavering. Mannelli bristled, rising to the bait: "Obviously I would rather no one died, Miss. And you are right, my job is no more difficult than catching a very dangerous man. To protect and serve." Mannelli said simply. His gaze went to the camera and the screen cut to one of those news friendly spin doctors, offering his two cents:

"We live in a media society, we've all seen the movies, read the books. *Silence of The Lambs, Seven,* and *Kiss The Girls.* Sociopaths are the modern disease. We take murderers and put their faces on t–shirts. We glorify them. Turn them into heroes. Everyone gets their fifteen minutes of fame, but the truth, the ugly truth, is that we don't need movies to embroider the sicknesses inherent in men. Men like The Trinity Killer are more frightening than anything Hollywood can conjure because they are real…"

He paused to let the weight of his words sink and the inset image of Mannelli at the press conference to fade.

"They are real…They are frightening. Men devoid of care or compassion. Oblivious to feelings of guilt and conscience, the things that keep normal people in line. A thrill seeker busy chasing down the highest high, no matter what the cost. Always ready, eager, to face the rapidly escalating risks involved in what they are doing. They don't care. There is no guilt. No remorse."

And cut into adverts. Beauty and fashion to distract the world from its obsession with fear and loathing.

BRENDON Ellery, Manhattan District's Chief Coroner tapped out the all too familiar set numbers, listening to the jangle of the bell at the other end of the line.

He was alone in the mortuary, the last assistant long gone for an overdue lunch. Midway through the fourth bleat the ringing abruptly died and Bill Stern's cigar–husked baritone answered:

"Stern, homicide."

"Could I speak with Lieutenant Mannelli?"

"Sorry, the boss is tied up with the scavengers at the minute, can I take a message?"

"This is Brendon Ellery."

"Hey, what's up Doc?" Stern cut across him, trying to sound like Bugs Bunny but managing something close to Pee Wee Herman. "Miss me that much you just had to call?"

"Very good, Detective. Look, can you tell Mannelli I think we might have a bigger problem on our hands than any of us bargained for." He heard the voice on the other end of the open line suck in a sharp whistle of breath and imagined him shaking his head. "Have you got the Scott girl's file in front of you?"

There was a muffled rifle of papers, followed by, "Yup, found her."

"Good. You see she suffered a severe amount of cranial trauma, fractured skull, manubrium and sternum caved in, costal cartilage torn, universal lesions, discoloration and damage to the spinal vertebra, yes? That's not counting the knife wounds."

The answer had come to him after Stern had left to answer the call to Riverside. It seemed so bloody obvious now, that he wondered how he could have missed it for so long. Looking at things head on...its like the Chinese finger puzzles, the harder you pull at the idea the less chance you have of finding what you are looking for...you just end up trapped and pulling against yourself. Now, that rings familiar with what we know about the Matther girl and to a lesser extent Caroline Öberg, am I right?"

"I guess..." Stern conceded uncertainly.

"Good. But you'll notice that the other files show either a marked absence or severely lessened degree of physical damage. The cause of death throughout appears to be asphyxiation as opposed to hemorrhaging or penetrations, yes? And the tattoos are present on all bodies," Ellery paused, waiting for the cent to drop and the sobering effect of his words to set in.

"I'm not sure I see where you're going with this, Doc?"

"Think about it then. What would be the worst–case scenario you could dream up for this Trinity Killer of yours?"

Stern didn't need to think too hard. "More than one," he said somberly.

"Yes. That's where I am going, detective. If I am right, and I have a very strong suspicion that I am, the nine bodies brought in so far have been killed by different people. Similar if not identical murders but almost definitely the work of different men. The bitterest irony being that they have been telling us this from the start, with their Holy Trinity. Father D'Angelo's body just helped to confirm things. It's like one of the killers has, and I know it is a bad word under the circumstances, but it's like one of the Trinity has an element of style, panache, call it what you will. He has a penchant for killing and takes a certain amount of pride in what he's doing. The remainder of the Trinity is simply churning out results to a set formula. Quicker, and more brutal. Definitely got a taste for the macabre if you consider the mutilations. I just can't decide if they are working in concert, knowingly, or independently."

Stern was silent for a moment.

"You don't think he might have been hurried or something? You know, disturbed or caught in the act, so to speak?"

Ellery exhaled a labored breath and shook his head, not that Stern could appreciate the gesture down the phone line. "It's possible of course, anything is possible, but not likely, I'm afraid. The more I think about it, the surer I am we have to face up to an ugly reality."

Across the city, Bill Stern said, "Thanks Doc," biting down the frustration until the phone was back in its cradle. Then he punched the concrete wall.

"Shitshitshitshitshit."

nineteen

DELGADO noticed three things as he moved up the stairs in the high-rise apartment overlooking the Hudson.

The first, that he was way, way out of shape and needed to do something about it. The second, that if he didn't deal with the first one real soon, The Job would kill him before he had the chance to set matters right. And third, that there was a God-awful stink hanging in the air around him; and he didn't like any one of them all that much.

One way or another, Jack Delgado had spent too much of his life in death rooms, in hospitals, houses and crime scenes, and he knew well enough the special attar that clung to them like lovers. That smell of feces, urine and decay crawled down the twisting stairwell, happy to greet him as he walked in.

All of a sudden he really didn't want to be the one that opened the door; he'd been that person for all of his twenty-four years on the force and now he wanted nothing more from his life than to let other people do the door opening and the cleaning up.

He heard quiet, muffled sobbing coming from somewhere above and took it as a sign that the neighbor had stuck around and was maybe a little more than just a neighbor. Wheezing slightly and short of breath, Delgado rounded the final twist of stairs and peered along the short corridor.

In the corner, beyond the second of two doors, hunched a dirty looking man—boy, he amended. Hair clung to his damp scalp in lank ringlets, framing his pinched features, and Delgado saw, when he looked up, the black circles around the boy's gaunt, harrowed eyes and the streaks of cried-out tears.

Reaching into his pocket, he pulled out his wallet and flipped it open to show the boy his ID.

"Delgado, NYPD," he deliberately substituted the final word, homicide. It wouldn't help the kid to know who had drawn the departmental short straw.

The boy sniffed, wiping a hand across his wet cheek as he tried to pull himself together. He pushed himself unsteadily to his feet.

Jesus, Delgado thought, *he's only a kid.* And then he thought, *I don't want to do this...I really don't want to do this.*

But he did it anyway.

Stooping, he levered the mailbox open with his fingers and, putting his cheek against the burnished bronze of the flap, put his eye to it.

The smell was there.

Waiting beyond the door was another room where death had danced her merry jig.

There was only one thing left for Jack Delgado to do, and that was open the door.

Well, here goes nothing...

He tried the handle.

Locked.

He looked at his watch: no time to go chasing down the landlord for his master key, even less time to scare up a warrant and keep the etiquette mongers at Internal Affairs happy. *Life and death,* he told himself with a wry smile. And made a judgment call.

Putting his shoulder against the wood he rocked back on the balls of his feet. Slammed his shoulder against the door. The wood groaned inwards, slightly, but otherwise didn't give an inch. The lock held firm and his shoulder screamed out its agony as a bright flare of pain hammered through the bone.

Reaching back inside his pocket Delgado pulled out his .38 special, aimed at the lock and fired a single shot; mingling cordite with the stagnant aroma of death. Putting his shoulder to the door this time, the wood around the lock mechanism splintered sharply as it gave way, and the door swung in on itself.

The smell...

Holding an off–white handkerchief over his mouth and nose, Delgado edged his way in.

Inside wasn't the charnel house the stench threatened. Indeed, at first sight nothing was amiss. Only the fetid smell gave way to the lie. Oddly, Delgado found himself drawing conclusions about the woman he knew was here somewhere. Nothing was out of place. No laundry rested on the backs of chairs in the bedroom. No deodorant sprays lay topless on the counters in the bathroom. No lather–soaked disposable razors resting in the sink trough. No empty fast–food trays in the kitchen.

Turning his back on the kitchen, he moved through to the lounge again. Still, nothing looked out of place, but the smell was strongest in here. This was the death room.

He looked around again.

The blinds were twisted shut on the view, clogging the afternoon sun. The furniture, a new looking leather set, two two–seater couches and a bucket seat, were lined up against the back wall, a coffee table sat in front of the sofa. A large flat–screen tv and sleeklined Nicam video and the loops of its coaxial aerial cable looping back across the floor dominated one corner, a desk and Macintosh Powerbook, another.

Behind him, Delgado heard the boy enter the room.

He was crying again; low, moaning sobs stifled by the hand he held across his face.

Turning, Delgado made a shrugging gesture, as if to say: your guess is as good as mine...

And the boy screamed.

Delgado swung fully around, eyes darting left and right, looking.

What the–?

All too quickly he saw why.

A leg, twisted impossibly out of shape by the double–sided press of the wall and the back of the sofa stood awkwardly on a shattered ankle. As far as Delgado could tell, it wasn't attached to a body. A caked puddle of muddy brown stained the white carpet around the bare foot. Dried blood clung in a twisting streetmap of meshed lines across the discolored skin.

Three seats down, a second leg hung likewise, impossibly twisted, fully seven feet away from the first.

GABRIEL stood beneath the bushy canopy of the wistful old willow beside Celine's graveside, sucking smoke from his thin brown–skinned roll–up. Her name, Charlotte Annuci, lettered in gold on the gray marble. He wore a long black raincoat that slicked off the steady city rain and a wide–brimmed black felt fedora that obscured most of his face.

Wisps of smoky cloud drifted across his shadowy features, diffusing into the heavy air like lacy ghosts.

Why didn't you believe me…? I tried to tell you…I tried…

St. Vincent's was a gritty little cemetery backing onto Riverside Park. Chain–linked wire fences bordered the sodden grass. Behind the fences white–walled Neo–Gothic structures climbed towards the gray sky, casting their pale shadows over the desolate tombstones.

Across from the regimented rows of lackluster graves a thick column of gray–black smoke billowed free of the crematorium's bulbous chimney, staining the dull sky.

Reaching inside his coat to fish out another brown–skinned cigarette he found himself remembering her face, but when he saw her it was like looking at a jigsaw with a piece missing and the more he tried to focus on that missing something, the more he started to lose it. Gabriel rolled the thin cigarette between his fingers and stuck it between his lips. He lit up, the lambent glow of the flame casting wraithlike shadowdancers across his face, then capped the lighter and slipped it back into his pocket. She was going.

Soon, she'll be gone altogether and who'll be crying for her then?

He knelt, taking a rose from inside the raincoat, and laid it in front of the sullen headstone.

"I might forget what you look like, Celine…Charlotte, but I won't forget to put roses on your grave. I promise. I won't forget that."

Gabriel stood and walked slowly away, haunted by the music of the rain and the excited laughter of a three–year–old boy. "I can hear you, Sammy…I can hear you."

ANOTHER gravestone. The empty space was heart–piercingly cold, the first snows of Christmas falling from the sky. In those clouds Gabriel saw the faces of yesterday, his dead looking down on him from on high.

He knelt, took a small metal dump truck from his pocket, and laid it at the foot of his son's grave, beside a plastic Indian, dead boy's curls of paint flaking away from the shaft of the Black Foot's tomahawk.

"I miss you, you know, kiddo. I miss you so much." He felt arms that weren't there wrap around his shoulders, drawing him into a gentle embrace. "It's not fair, Frankie, it's not fair…"

No, it never is.

"Why though? What did he do?" Gabriel swallowed, wiping his eyes with the back of a trembling hand. "Why didn't I die? Why? When you died, why didn't I die? I didn't want to be left behind…"

The wind carried the lullaby of her breaking voice: *Hush little baby, don't say a word…* The commitment in her imagined voice was a haunting reminder of a midnight promise gone sour. The perfect, unkeepable promise of love everlasting.

Wiping a hand across his broken face, Gabriel stood shakily. "God, why do I miss you so very, very much?"

For that one, the wind had no answer he wanted to hear.

Without looking up from his feet he walked back to the Studebaker.

HE drove with the window cranked open, letting the steady feed of iced air onto his face keep him awake; letting it keep the ghosts away.

Leaning down, Gabriel hunted either end of the dial for something worth listening to, settling for the loud backslash of freeform jazz piano over the dull threnody of Declan Shea's scratchy voice.

He had nowhere to go, but somedays nowhere wasn't such a bad place to be, so he just drove, through the stretching towers of concrete and glass scraping through the thickening flakes of snow; and on every snowflake a ghost of the past came riding down. Places they'd shared. Every building had its ghost, every street corner its memory.

The Studebaker was bleeding a fine tail of oil behind itself, like a snail in the early morning.

Satellite dishes and antenna broke out like acne on the face of the city.

In his head, or in the passenger seat, Francesca cradled their son in her arms, her long fingers tangling in the boy's mop of dark hair, soothing Sam into a second pair of arms and the embrace of sleep. She was singing, *Hush little baby, don't say a word, Daddy's gonna buy you a mocking bird, and if that mocking bird won't sing, daddy's gonna buy you a diamond ring...*

Tears in his eyes, Gabriel had to stop the car. Cars went past on the outside, their horns braying, inside his heart was breaking.

THE colors danced with a secret life all of their own.

Secret.

Magic and beauty.

A house of mirrors, where everything was all there was.

Truths whispered out of the mouths of babes; white rabbits plucked from the conjurer's hat; sticky gossamer strands tailored by the spider of life; dreams left undreamed. Truths whispered from the mouths that swallowed from bottles wrapped in brown paper bags, smoked other peoples' discarded dog–ends and talked to garbage cans claiming to hear the voice of God coming from within.

Secrets secret.

Green the color of the grass ran into yellow and into orange, blurring with a lack of distinction around the fringes where emotions frayed and crossed; blue into indigo, indigo into purple into red into black. Into decay.

And that was where he lived.

Where the Colors danced.

The lone spectator of the Color Dance, over the last days he had often found himself wondering: Why me? Why am I blessed with this curse? But he knew the answer, because he was a Dancer and of all the Colors he was Red.

Red was his color as much as he was its; Red for hate, for anger, hurt and pride. Red for lust and avarice and degradation. Red for pain, for greed; of pain, of hate, of anger, of lust, of want, of need, of hate...of pain...

But most of all, of people.

If only they knew...

Yes, he was The Trinity. Yes, he was Red. A few more days, a few more miracles and they would know his name. The need would be satisfied and he could walk into Black. The no–color. Black, where death could undo his immortal soul, free him from this hell of his own making.

THE Trinity Killer sat on the edge of Prospect Park Lake, his bare feet trailing in the cool blue.

Thinking.

His thoughts composed of a single colorful dream: Visions of composing the ultimate lullaby, leading his fellow Dancers through the bloody streets, ribbons of hate streaming in his wake, the spider's web of death dancing around his feet as he spun and swirled though the wilderness of glass.

On the grass, the Village Voice's bold headline was a noose around his neck, tightening: the Pontiac, it had been a mistake, his first, leaving it like that. He hadn't been thinking.

He looked up again at the fountain–like plume of scintillating glass reaching out of the frozen lake, its eddying twists and minute enclaves of sky–catching crystal attracting and absorbing the failing light. Beyond the reach of the supplicating edifice, the surface of Prospect Park Lake, edge to distant edge, had crusted over with a film of red glass flimsy enough to ripple with the caress of the choked inner–city breeze.

He rocked slightly on his buttocks, arms around his knees, just rocking, rocking, drawing comfort from the simple movement.

The world of glass in the failing light, sight and image diffused around the column of angry redness beneath the glass skin of reality, which it somehow reflected back into the gathering twilight, its body a thousand thousand angry fireflies hovering under the influence of a single malevolent mind. Manhattan's tower of hate. Every city had one, its angry manhood eager to fuck with all the pretty pretties...

This was the coming of the time between times, between day and night, night and day, when the Guardians of The Dance could tread the streets in certain safety, quietly choreographing the moves needed to make up the next unearthly scene.

The Trinity Killer, an angel bathed in red, folded the newspaper and stood up, a film of crack–iced glass freezing the grass under his bare feet and spreading out from the pivot toward the line of thick–trunked oak and spruce less than a hundred meters from his lakeside seat. In seconds, the crucified scarecrows, behind which the failing sun was slowly melting into a languid twilight, were nothing more than bones of coruscating glass, skeletal arms clawing at the sky, sparkling against the halo of the dying sun, catching and reflecting the whole spectrum of colors whilst somehow radiating only a sickly red tinge.

Around him ghostly slivers of red dazzled, catching and replicating the reflections thrown down on the mirror trees by the darkening sky.

The screams of his dead, desperate shrieking, pitches rising and falling in the single voice of terror rang out across the twilight park, as impossible as the dancer's walking corpse. Pulses of red light came in waves, radiating off the central plume of glass out in the center of the lake, spreading outwards in tight ripples, each pulse accompanied by the lament of a tortured soul, a scream from dead lips.

Almost exactly as the voices finally fell quiet, the crimson light within the glass pillar snuffed out, leaving behind a single, curiously iridescent vapor that curled away from the base of the shaft.

What they could find out about a man six months dead, he failed to see. Carlos Lamenzo, the whispered Trinity, stared down at his bloody hands, as dead now as he had been that summer night six months ago when the Angel stepped down from its perch among the Cherubim around the crucifixion display nailed by its glass heart to the wall above the votive candles in St. Malachy's, and poured its twisted soul into his empty husk, breathed life where before there was nothing except the black of death.

That was the Secret of The Dance, and that was his secret as much as it was the Color's. His and his Angel's, now that they were one and the same. That was why the Angel of Red had wound its cord so far, through the maze of twists and turns of the Otherworldly City, so far from the safety of the crystal tree to be beside, inside, its dancer.

He could feel the stirrings, the sympathetic pangs of need clawing at his stomach walls. Nothing in the world could have prepared him for this...Pain...

Wiping his hands off on his jeans, Lamenzo reached into his back pocket for the folded scrap of newspaper, the last grizzly souvenir of life before. It said little, a few lines in memoriam of a family cut down brutally. Multiple homicide. He knew the truth behind the words like no one else possibly could. After all, it was his story.

A woman, wreathed in a veil of pineapple yellow and jade green jogged by, ponytail bouncing lightly as her feet danced across the span of the wooden bridge, ignorant of the miracles flowering all around her.

The Trinity Killer watched her pass with eyes of fire, burning hot and so achingly cold, watched her pass...

twenty five

MANNY Bossman's small family delicatessen cupped the corner of a southern Bronx street. Its plate windows, wearing the neatly hand-painted logo 'The Boss Man's Deli,' faced north and east, onto the jungle.

That street corner sat on the edge of Crack Alley, one of the worst neighborhoods in the Bronx; by night it belonged to the winos, bag ladies, junkies, and crazies who dragged themselves out of their holes with the setting of the sun.

It cultivated its own stink too, like so many other street corners abandoned by night to the lowlife; the odor of forest green garbage sacks split by grubbing claws; the odor of boxes, bottles and cans strung out through the gaping holes; the odor of piss and puke.

It was a bad place to live, even before his beloved Thelma had been taken up to Jehovah. Only nostalgia and guilt kept the street corner store open during the darkest days; memories of Thelma, of their two children, Jesse and Katarina, and now the grandchildren, Rosie and Stephen. In both, Manny saw the familiar spirit of his wife. Her ghost, it seemed, refused to rest; and guilt that he had fallen asleep and somehow allowed his neighborhood to slip so low.

In the last hour of daylight, before closing up for the night, Manny Bossman shuffled about the gas-lit store, sliced salami, pastrami and liverwurst for tomorrow, wiped down spotless counters and stainless slicers, and polished the long strip mirror that ran the length of the back wall.

Three streets away, in St. Malachy's, Carlos Lamenzo made his excuses to Father Joseph D'Angelo, flimsy as they were, and made to leave.

As always, he paused between the Narthex and the Nave, dipped two fingers into the font, his reflection shimmering in the cool blue of the marble basin, crossed himself hurriedly with holy water and bowed his head before the flickering flames of the half dozen votive candles and spotlight illuminated crucifix above the altar.

He dashed out into the smells of Hart Street, his own heart racing as he skirted the litter-strewn edge of Castle Hill Park and ducked back into the mire of Castle Hill Avenue.

Barbis and the others were waiting for him outside the entrance to the subway. The attar of Henry Barbis' cheap cologne hung heavily in the July air. The boarded–up houses along this particular stretch of slum land all looked similarly dreary. The streetlamp outside the station was off, the bulb shattered and not replaced. The curtains of the houses on either side of the station were drawn. It was that time, when people stopped peering out between the drapes to check on the aimlessly milling kids. A couple of doors down a dog growled, but the four men ignored it, waiting for Barbis' lead.

As if to some silent signal, he began walking unhurriedly toward the darkened alley traversing Cicero and Caesar, the big man's abnormally crooked gait trailing his two–tone spats across the concrete sidewalk. The others moved cautiously behind him.

"What's he up to?" Lamenzo whispered to the Bantam–sized Latino at his side, meaning their self–elected leader.

Jimmy Ortega looked at him, his usually playful eyes unreadable in the gloom, and shrugged his butterfly shoulders. "Prick reckons he's got himself a line into Rodriguez," his voice, coated with a Spanish accent, whispered back. Ortega smiled crookedly. "Seems like he's willing to put some bigger business our way if we do okay tonight. No fuck–ups and maybe he'll even let us in on a crack–house run."

"Yeah? You're not shittin' me are ya?"

"Why the fuck would I, man?"

"Shit, he's gotta be out of his fuckin' head mixing up with a motherfucker like Tony Rodriguez."

"Too fuckin' right, my man. But he reckons the shit's worth it."

"How 'bout you?"

"Me?" Ortega seemed genuinely amused by the thought. "What the fuck's it matter what I think? You think ol' Henry'd listen to what I think?" The young Chicano sneered and spat into the gutter.

"Where we goin' then?"

"Gotta put the squeeze on some old Jewboy, seems like he's not coughin' up the insurance on time and Rodriguez is gettin' real pissed with him."

"No shit?"

"Yeah, no shit…Just like the fuckin' movies huh?"

"Just like the fuckin' movies," Lamenzo agreed.

Barbis had slipped out of the alley, drawing the others with him like flies. The houses along this side of Caesar all looked the same, terraced and semi–detached rowhouses, unremarkable houses lived in by unremarkable people.

People like Manny Bossman.

The old man's street corner delicatessen stood in darkness, the only light the spectral black–and–white glow of the television set coming through the glass of one of the small upper windows.

Barbis stopped, tilting his head upwards until the television's glow touched his scowling features. The knife he drew from his belt was about eight inches long, serrated along a single edge, and wickedly sharp.

Lamenzo didn't hurry to catch up. Instead he loitered around the entrance onto the street, kicking unconsciously at the forest of municipal garbage sacks lining the gutter, spilling chicken bones and potato peels with his feet.

Eddie Morreno and Jimmy Ortega moved up to stand side by side at Barbis' shoulder, their eyes echoing his, lifting to join his in a curbside vigil.

"Time for work, boys," Barbis purred, a coarse crack from his bruised knuckles punctuating each short word.

Morreno took his cue. Edging past the still grinning Barbis, he tried the main door. Not surprisingly, it was locked. "S'locked," he grumbled, needlessly stating the obvious as he stepped back from the door.

Barbis' pencil–thin lips twisted into a wry smile as he nodded to Ortega. "Around the side, Jimmy."

"No problem," Ortega agreed, squatting down and pulling a knife of his own from a hidden boot–sheath. The little Chicano disappeared around the side of the building.

Lamenzo walked forward, careful not to make a sound, until he drew level with Barbis and Morreno. "What're we gonna do to the old guy?"

"Just rough him up a bit, Carlos. You know the deal. Rodriguez wants him frightened and we're frightening," Barbis answered softly.

"There's not gonna be no blood is there, Henry? I've got to be back to help Father Joe with the evening service, remember."

"No blood, I promise you, Carlos," Barbis breathed in his ear. "No blood."

Hidden until the last moment by shadow, Jimmy Ortega made his way back to the others. "There's a metal fire escape around the back," he whispered, breathing hard. "Only goes as far as the second floor, but there's a fly–window up there that shouldn't be too much trouble."

"What are we waiting for?" Lamenzo asked dryly.

The four men moved cautiously along the narrow walkway until Ortega gestured for them to stop. "This is it," he whispered, pointing at the peeling face of an oddly colorless gate. "Just watch the step, 'kay?"

If before they were quiet, crossing the killing ground between the colorless gate and the fire escape at the rear of The Boss Man's Deli they were church mice.

A rusted garbage bin stood close by, under the swinging legs of the escape's ladder, at least eight feet above. Eddie Morreno pushed it aside with his foot, ignoring the protesting screech of metal as it grated against the chipped concrete of the yard. He smiled broadly and squatted down, clasping his hands together to form a stirrup.

"Would you be so kind as to do the honors?" Barbis whispered to Ortega, nodding down at the kneeling shadow of Eddie Morreno.

"My pleasure." Jimmy Ortega put his foot on the helping hands and allowed himself to be boosted up until his questing fingers snagged on the first rung of the metal ladder, then pulled himself up until his swinging feet caught the base of that first precious rung. He danced up the remaining rungs until he emerged on the narrow, rusting platform, from where he could reach the small fly–window he had talked about. Without waiting to be told, Ortega slid the thin blade of his knife into the frame of the window, working the point up and down carefully until the window latch finally came loose. He nudged it gently with the side of his clenched fist, popping it open.

Ortega paused for a moment, listening, then swung himself inside.

The sounds of a distant television crept down the bare flight of stairs, reaching his ears as he lowered himself down onto the boards. He stood on the darkened stairs, waiting for the others to join him.

Lamenzo was first, Barbis next, Morreno last, maneuvering

with remarkable dexterity for a man of his size. He clambered through the window as Ortega made to move a step further toward the dimly phosphorescent landing. He too could hear the sounds coming from above.

Henry Barbis chewed on his bottom lip, contemplating the savagery of the next move, his expression of confusion gradually melting into a broad grin of satisfaction. He looked at Ortega and nodded, gesturing silently towards the faint light.

Lamenzo made to give way, letting both Barbis and Morreno step past him.

Both men paused on the landing, Barbis looking left, Morreno right, ignoring the ribbon of gray light seeping under the nearest door. Jimmy Ortega reached for the handle.

It opened soundlessly, the blue–white light trapped within slithering out to wash over Ortega's Latino features. The musical call of the television was louder now, droning and muttering, occasionally breathing a whisper of song.

It was playing to itself.

The old man was asleep in his chair.

MANNY watched the end credits roll, their hypnotic vertical dance drawing *The Bold and The Beautiful* to a close. He didn't feel much like moving, even to the point of bearing the bland commercials and the soporific dancing girls selling life insurance.

There hadn't been so much as a squeak from Rosie's room all night, not that he ever had trouble with her. Normally Stephen was the light sleeper, but he was off with his father this time. As ever, Rosie simply collapsed with exhaustion, all played out two minutes after lights–out, leaving Manny to tuck her tiny feet under the blankets and smooth the lustrous bangs of thick auburn hair from her untroubled brow; the same lovely shade of dark red–brown, like cherrywood, as her mother. Both children had the same gold–touched skin, but because Rosie's eyes were a shade greener than her older brother's, her features were that shade more appealing.

At six, she was all that he could handle, at sixteen she'd be melting hearts.

Finally, indulging thoughts of hot cocoa, Manny Bossman dozed off, old bones happy to settle down for the night just where they were...

HE was only half asleep when the frigid hand grabbed him by the throat and hauled him backwards, strong fingers constricting his windpipe like pincers, killing any attempt at a scream. At least he thought it was a hand. It felt like the flesh of a week–dead eel, cold and damp with the first dank touch of decay. It stank, too. Not much, but enough. The redolent musk of too much cheap cologne, so bitter and sharp that even in small whiffs it was too much to take.

Still dazed and half sleep–blind, Manny Bossman was yanked upright, the strength behind the hands almost lifting him out of the seat.

Something felt cold against his cheek.

More fingers?

No.

Henry Barbis pressed the serrated edge of the razor–sharp blade against the concertinaed folds of old man's flesh gathered beneath Manny's jaw and breathed in his ear: "So much as breathe, Jewboy, and I'll cut you fuckin' head off, comprende?"

Manny tried to swallow but his throat was as dry and burned out as the Mojave. He closed his eyes, dark crow's feet creasing in the parched skin. Sniffed, trying to fight back the tears but losing.

There was laughter now, slow, cold and cynical. Manny Bossman blinked his teary eyes open, mustering his defiance, and looked up, biting down the urge to whimper and plead.

There were three that he could see; with the hands around his throat, that made four. He held the eyes of each, his gaze level, searching for some trace of compassion.

There was none.

"Got a message from Tony Rodriguez," Barbis whispered in his ear, his breath a low, rattling wheeze. "Eddie, if you'd be so kind…" Releasing his hold on the old man's throat, Barbis grabbed a handful of silver–gray hair and yanked his head back, the point of the knife never straying far from his cheekbone.

Sadness and fear warred within him. He wished for death, right then, rather than the realization of things to come, but death didn't have a place in the delicatessen; not yet.

Eddie Morreno took a slow step forward, staring directly into the old man's face, his brutish eyes a void lacking expression beyond the simple need, hunger.

Manny's guts cramped as Morreno's fist smashed into his left side, pulled back, hammered in again. And again.

"Enough?" Barbis drawled into Manny's ear, easing his grip on the old man's hair, letting an inch slip through his fingers as the old man's head sagged, lolling and rolling on his neck. The little resistance offered by his body sapped by body blows. Barbis jerked his head up again, for Eddie Morreno to pummel his fist into, bludgeoning bone and cartilage into submission under a torrential rain of merciless blows.

"What...what do you want?" He lisped the words dully, between swollen lips and bloodied teeth.

"Everything, man," Barbis leered. "But for now, money. You give us the money coming to Rodriguez and we won't hurt you anymore. It's that simple, grandpa."

The knife was back at his cheek, pressing harder than before, betraying the lie beneath Henry Barbis' sugar–coated words.

"Oh, oh Jesus...there isn't any money. Please, you've got to believe me. There isn't any money..."

"I don't know...You believe him, Jimmy?" Barbis asked mildly.

"Uh–hunh," Ortega shook his head, playing along to Barbis' tune.

"How about you, Eddie? You believe the Jewboy?"

"Uh–hunh," Morreno echoed Ortega, shaking his head.

"That only leaves Father Carlos. You think he's shittin' us, Father C?"

"Sure seems that way to me," Lamenzo said thoughtfully.

"Sure does, don't it," Barbis agreed, his tone bordering on contempt. "You want to see if you can't persuade him to be a bit more co–operative, Eddie?"

"Anything you say, Henry." Stepping forward again, Eddie Morreno interlaced his bulldog fingers and, one by one, cracked his knuckles for effect before ramming a blow into Manny Bossman's brittle ribs; cracking at least two, maybe as many as four.

The old man doubled up, gagging and gasping for breath.

Just like the fuckin' movies, Lamenzo thought bitterly.

"Now," Barbis hissed, "You aren't gonna be a dumbfuck and give us any more trouble are ya?"

Manny tried to shake his head but it was as if the last punch had severed the nerve endings along his spine and left him paralyzed from the waist up. He felt himself swoon and thought he was going to pass out.

"Grampa?" came a plaintive call from down the hall.

All five of them heard it.

"Who else is in the house," Barbis snarled, a bewildered crease curling his lips into a frown.

"She's only a child," Manny Bossman sobbed.

"Go get her, Father C," he ordered.

Lamenzo moved out into the unlit hall.

"Please...don't hurt her," the old man pleaded before Barbis clamped a hand across his mouth. The overbearing stench of cologne dragged a gagged retch from his constricted throat.

"Don't worry, he's good with kids." Barbis sneered, touching the point of the knife to the sack under his eye, allowing a salty droplet to dribble onto the blade. "Especially little ones..."

Lamenzo paused on the landing, listening for more calls, then, slowly, he began to move towards the only door standing slightly ajar. He saw the little girl sitting upright in bed as he opened the door, the blue–white backlight silhouetting him like a cheap cinema effect. "Hello," he said softly.

"Who are you?" Rosie asked, smiling up at him with all the innocence he could stand, her green eyes haunting him.

"A friend of your Grampa's," he soothed, kneeling beside her, "What's your name, Angel?"

"Rosie," she told him.

"That's a pretty name, Angel. A real pretty name."

"What's Grampa doing?" Rosie asked, folding her legs up and tucking them in under her small bottom so she sat higher in the bed.

"Nothing, Angel. He's just having a chat with a few friends. You know how he is once he gets going. I'm sorry if we woke you."

"Okay," she said sleepily. "Will you get Grampa to come in and give me a kiss please?"

"Sure, Angel. You sit tight, snuggle down and I'll get him to come in. Okay?"

"Yeah," she yawned, stretching and cuddling down beneath the covers again.

Lamenzo leaned down, brushed an errant strand of cherry-wood hair away and planted a soft kiss on her forehead.

"Night–night," Rosie mumbled, her eyes already closed.

"Goodnight, Angel."

Smiling, Lamenzo backed out of the room.

"Where's the kid?" Barbis wanted to know as he walked into the lounge. The old man was slumped in his chair, a bubble of bloody snot pulsing, smaller and bigger, under a flared nostril. Blue–black welts and bruises marked his chalk–white complexion, reminders of Eddie Morreno's fists. He looked up at Lamenzo, grief and humiliation swelling in his rheumy eyes.

"You didn't...didn't hurt her?" he pleaded, whimpering and clawing pathetically.

"Sure is a pretty lil thing, ain't she?" Lamenzo snickered, hunkering down beside the old man.

"Is she...?"

"She's sleeping like a babe. Gave me a goodnight kiss too. Sweet kid."

Manny whimpered, the bubble of caked snot bursting over his lip. He turned to Barbis again. "What do you want? I'll give you anything, please don't hurt Rosie, please...she's only a baby..."

The girl, the girl, Rosie...the words buzzed frantically inside Lamenzo's head.

"The money. All we want is the money."

"Oh God...there...there's no money...you've got to believe me..."

"Man, you fuckin' Jews are tight..." Barbis tutted, shaking his head. "Don't jerk me off, fuckhead. Give me the fuckin' money or so help me God, I'll rip the fuckin' kids heart out with my fuckin' teeth!"

"Please God...you've got to believe me...there is no money..."

"One more time, old man. One more time." Barbis warned.

"There isn't..."

"GET ME THE FUCKIN' KID, EDDIE. NOW!"

It happened so fast Morreno didn't have time to move. Barbis whirled on the old man and hurled his hunting knife, the hilt catching him above the right eye, the blade plunging into the foam stuffing of the high–backed armchair, quivering.

Barbis slipped a hand inside his jacket and smoothly drew a gun, training its black eye on one of Manny Bossman's. "Where's the money, motherfucker! Where's the fuckin' money!" he screamed, spittle flecks spraying with each word. He thrust the pistol under Manny's chin, pushing it up until the old man whimpered against the pain.

Somehow, Bossman shook his head.

"No money..."

Instead of squeezing off a shot, Barbis backhanded the barrel across his jaw. The pain was immediate, the touch of death close at hand. A second backhanded slap of metal caught him just above the eye, ripping a gash from eyebrow to hairline. A third smashed his eye closed.

He fell back, the room dissolving under a spray of red, felt himself being kicked and dragged until the floor fell away and he knew he was dead. Wooden daggers slashed out under him while walls bludgeoned him. He tried to cry out but nothing came.

The cessation of rolling blows told him he had hit the bottom, and then the hands were on him again.

Blood stung his blind eyes as he tried to see where he was, and what was being done to him. His body burned in a thousand places. Through the bloodied veneer of blindness he heard one of them laugh, another say "Loser," and another sound, impossible to dislocate from the countless sensations stabbing at him through the dark.

At the base of the stairs, kneeling over Manny Bossman's unmoving body, Barbis thumbed back the hammer, jammed the pistol's fluted muzzle between the chipped, yellow stained teeth in the old man's gaping mouth and pumped the trigger three times in quick succession.

The short but deafening cacophony ruptured the delicatessen.

Manny Bossman lay in a whorish sprawl, legs splayed, trousers kinked up around his thighs; his body looked like a slumped scarecrow, blood and brains leaking in streamers from the rent in the back of his skull, splashing across the tiled floor.

On the landing, Carlos Lamenzo heard the shots and realized he was screaming. His stomach muscles clenched, the bile in his throat souring at the thought of what kind of damage a .45 caliber bullet would have done to the old man close up. It would literally have taken his head off.

Behind him, the child was screaming.

Downstairs, Henry Barbis threw his head back and laughed.

"What the fuck'd ya wanna go an' do that for man?" Lamenzo heard Ortega protesting, his nasal Spanish whine shrill in the suddenly cemeterial darkness below.

Outside, the twilight was fading rapidly into night. The remaining luster a purplish veil clinging to some objects more than others, providing only vague suggestions of the grotesqueries slumped and spilled at the base of the stairs, managing to make the threats below more mysterious and more obscure than they would have been in total darkness.

"Shut the fuck up, man. Shut the fuck up or I'll blow your fuckin' head off!" Barbis shrieked, wheeling around; the cold black eye of the gun falling level with an invisible point on Jimmy Ortega's troubled face.

There was madness in his eyes, cold, pure insanity, blazing.

Ortega looked deep into those mad eyes and for the first time saw the full effect of the seething hatred that dwelled behind them.

Lamenzo raised fingers to his face, to wipe the salt tears of sweat from his cheek. Only then did he see that his hand was shaking. He swallowed hard. Numb.

Rosie shrieked on, louder. Raw.

Shut up, Rosie, shut up, shut up, shut up...

"Hey man," he heard Jimmy Ortega protest a second before Barbis blew him backwards into the cold provisions counter, the weight of his fall shattering the glass frontage of the cabinet. His body slumped like a bloody, disjointed marionette, a raw gash of weeping muscle ripped through the hole where his right eye had stared, limbs collapsing in under themselves until he hit the floor.

Lamenzo closed his eyes. When he opened them again, Jimmy Ortega was dead.

"Anyone else? Huh? Anyone else got a fuckin' problem?" Barbis howled, wheeling manically this way and that, never allowing the gun's muzzle to fall below waist height.

"No, no...I ain't got no problems, Henry," Lamenzo heard Eddie Morreno blubbering through the layers of veiled darkness.

"What about you, Father C? You got a fuckin' problem with that?"

Oh, sweet Jesus...

"No," Lamenzo breathed, certain he was at the mercy of a madman. "No, I got no problems, Henry..."

"That's right, you ain't got no fuckin' problems with Uncle Henry! Now shut that fuckin' kid up, she's makin' me fuckin'

CRAZY…" Lamenzo heard the dry click of the hammer going back. "Shut that fuckin' screaming bitch up, man, or I'll blow your fuckin' balls off! You hear me? Shut the fuckin' bitch up!"

Lamenzo's mouth opened, with the exception of a vague gurgling sound nothing came out. His arms hung limply at his sides, fists clenching and relaxing spasmodically as dirt–ingrained fingernails burrowed into the soft pads of his rucked up palms, drawing blood.

Rosie had almost screamed herself out.

Almost, but not quite.

Not quite enough.

"Shut that fuckin' kid up, now!"

People must have heard something by now…even in a place like Crack Alley, gunshots carried…It was only a matter of time (it couldn't stand still) a matter of time before the mournful wailings of sirens rent the fabric of the night, minutes, seconds.

He was dead.

One way or another, he was dead.

They all were.

Rosie fell silent for a moment, and he thought he was saved, but she was only gathering a second wind. She continued shrieking, screaming, her burnt–out voice oscillating wildly; loud then soft, loud, then soft, echoing the imagined sirens just a few streets beyond hearing.

To Lamenzo's ears her terrified screams swelled beyond fear and confusion, reaching into teeth–jarring, bone–piercing pandemonium. He stood paralyzed on the landing, his hands pressed over his ears, waiting for the glasslike windows of his eyes to shatter.

"If you don't shut that fuckin' kid up I'm gonna shut you up! You hear me Carlos? You hear me? I'm gonna shut you up, fucker!"

"Please, Henry," he heard Eddie Morreno plead, and pictured the eye of the .45 sighting on the big man, opening a third eye in the center of his forehead…

Pictured the .45's bleak eye focusing on him.

But she's only a child for God's sake…

Don't think about it…

Do it…

Barbis you bastard…

You motherfucker…

Do it...

He reached for the door, easing it open and walked in.

Rosie was sitting up in bed without a tear in her bloodshot eyes. Her cheeks were all puffy and swollen with crying. The girl's screaming quietened as he knelt by her bedside. She glared at him in anger, confusion and defiance, no hint of fear in her green–red eyes.

"Calm down, Angel. No one's gonna hurt you. Father Carlos won't let no one hurt you," Lamenzo soothed, easing her down beneath the covers.

"W–what was all the banging?" she asked, sobbing.

"Just Henry, did he wake you, sugar?"

"What was he doing?"

"He tripped on the step and knocked Grampa's lamp down the stairs. Henry's real clumsy sometimes. Now you cuddle up, and I'll make sure nothing disturbs you again, okay?"

"Okay," she said, wriggling further down, under the blankets.

"There's a good girl," Lamenzo looked down at her, smiled and leaned across to kiss the top of her head. Whispered: "Sleep tight," as he reached under her head for the pillow. Jerked it around, over her face, his heavy hands pressing it down; smothering the child under their suffocating caress.

Her hands clawed at his, scratching and raking at his forearms as her legs bucked and thrashed underneath him, then relaxed, falling away limply as he choked off her will to fight.

He looked again at the child, barely able to make out her features through the darkness, illuminated as they were by the thinnest shaft of light coming through the mullioned window. She already looked dead, her green eyes open and staring at the ceiling, unable to accept the reality of what had just happened.

"Goodnight, sweet angel," he whispered, getting up to leave the room.

twenty eight

"MADE a piss–poor job of this, didn't we, Father C?" Barbis called, seeing Lamenzo appear at the head of the stairs.

"She isn't going to be a problem anymore, Henry." Lamenzo said, his voice flat and lacking intonation.

"Who ain't?"

"The girl."

"No problem. I like that. We ain't got no problems you and me Father C, huh? Me an' you man, we ain't got no problems...look, why don't you take a look see around upstairs, while me an' Eddie have a dig down here, there's got to be some fuckin' money here somewhere...right?"

He was in the lounge again, pulling out dresser drawers and dumping the jumbled contents on the floor, his fingers rifling through the scattered heaps of personal papers like some household vulture, scavenging for scraps, when he heard the forlorn wail of the first siren, still a distance away, followed by the distinctive sounds of breaking glass.

"Henry?" He called out, running onto the landing.

No answer.

The sirens were closer, close enough to be a problem.

He had three choices. Downstairs, side–stepping Manny Bossman's broken body and out into the street (passing Jimmy Ortega slumped against the cold meats counter, seeing the bloody hole gaping where his right eye ought to have been) and the hail of police gunfire.

Slipping out of the window, down the fire escape and away the way they'd come, through the gloom of the back alley and out, onto Cicero, back towards the sanctuary of St. Malachy's and Father Joe.

Or, sitting tight with the corpses and hitching a ride to the cemetery, care of a lethal injection.

He raced down the first flight of stairs, taking them two at a time, to the halfway landing, and clambered back out through the window, his feet clattering on the metal fire escape as they danced down the rungs. He jumped the last eight bone–jarring feet to the floor, sprawling, staggering, and running, his hands pitted and grazed with minute fragments of loose concrete and shale.

The yard was empty, the colorless gate swinging in the stygian gloom, its rusted hinges moaning. The night was still, suddenly threatening. The shadows bigger, cast by hulking concrete trees more statuesque than those rooted to the earth along the front street; they blocked out most of the light cast by the gibbous moon. There were a few streetlights, their puddles of amber light too widely spaced, separated by lakes of darkness.

A police siren.

Stroboscopic lights, red, black, red, black spun faster and faster.

Lamenzo charged out between the two gateposts, into the alley, into a patchwork of a thousand shadows, lights and sounds. Too many places to watch, things to see.

The sirens wailed away, continuously, madly.

Lamenzo cast a startled glance over his shoulder. Saw four of them.

They stood at the entrance to the alley, their legs apart, feet planted and arms raised, guns trained on his retreating back, less than thirty-five feet away. Blocking any hope of escape that way.

Another was crouched in the mouth of a gateway, a bullhorn held to his lips.

The end of the alley raced away from him, disappearing into the cavernous jaws of night, taking with it any hope.

"POLICE!" the static-distorted voice of the bullhorn holder hollered. "STOP RIGHT WHERE YOU ARE!"

Suppressing the nausea welling up from the pit of his stomach, Lamenzo made to run. He'd gone maybe five feet, veering left and right in a crazy zigzag across the blacktop when the muffled voice of the bullhorn shrieked again: "STOP RUNNING OR WE'LL SHOOT!"

Breathless, Lamenzo put his head down, running for all he was worth, passed the middle of the alley, out of the shadows, finding the vapor-thin sheen of moon-dappled light scattered across the street, expecting to hear the abrupt burst of gunfire come out of the dark, and feel the slugs punching into his back.

"REPEAT, STOP OR WE'LL SHOOT!"

Sounds.

Fear didn't allow him to slow his frantic pace.

When the first volley of gunfire ripped though the night, he instinctively ducked, felt something, like an autumnal breeze brush lightly over his head, and screamed as lead slammed into his shoulder.

He staggered away, moving blindly down the alley, finding another cluster of darkness, clawing at the thick, humid air with hooked fingers, his desperate veering run mirroring the mad capering of a rubber man.

"LAST TIME! STOP THROWING YOUR LIFE AWAY!"

Already have!

Damn you...

Already have...

Ignoring the stinging pain in his shoulder, Carlos Lamenzo ran on as best he could. The entrance onto Cicero was less than thirty paces, the end of the alley the same.

He only managed a few meters more before pulling up to an abrupt halt. Two bullets passed through his left leg, ripping open a ragged exit wound, one high in the thigh the other just above the knee; his dark, viscous blood spreading like a sunburst, darkening and staining the denim. His hands dropped, his knees buckling as he pitched forward another jerky step, his legs moving erratically under their own steam, pulling this way and that as if they were being manipulated by some drunken puppetmaster. He didn't crumple and fall to the ground but somehow straightened, his damaged knee locking and propelling him forward again.

Another bullet ripped into his right arm, leaving it hanging slackly at his side, his hand flopping and fluttering weakly.

The entrance onto Cicero waited less than fifteen steps away.

A slug took him low in the back, jerking his shoulders abruptly back. He lurched on another step, shuddering and convulsing as if a violent electric current flashed through his whole body.

Five steps from the Cicero road he weaved and slammed into a security fence, his knees giving out under him and pitching him towards the moonlit blacktop.

The pain superseded agony.

Sounds swarmed him, rushing through his watery eyes, bathing, lulling, like the swell of some midnight tide; his mother's voice, Father Joe's nasal burr, the thrumming vibration of cicadas' wings, the chirping of starlings, the mindless roar of engines, the bark of gunshots, screams; somewhere in there, Rosie Bossman's screams...

Little Rosie…

Oblivion threatened to overwhelm him, to undo him, but somehow he kept going, his legs lurching mechanically out onto Cicero.

Come on, Carlos, he screamed mentally, forcing himself onwards. It doesn't hurt! It doesn't hurt!

But it did hurt.

The pain in his left leg and lower back was incredible. He thought he could feel the blood running down his leg. He could definitely feel the slug in his spine squirming under his skin.

Screvin Avenue passed in a vortex of dizziness and nausea.

He must have blacked out on his feet because the next thing he knew, he was rounding off Barrett and onto Hart Street. Less than a hundred meters from St. Malachy's, his left leg flashed him a warning, just seconds before giving out on him. He could hear shouts somewhere, far away, and growing ever more distant beneath the swell of noise filling his ears.

Not long.

His vision swam in and out of focus. His lips were swollen, tongue stuck to the roof of his dry mouth and his throat burned. The muscles in his legs began to cramp, each footstep a giant step by feet encased in the frigid grip of concrete boots.

Somehow, he made it to the red brick steps of St. Malachy's. He had no recollection of the last hundred meters. Gasping, doubled over, with fire burning through his back, his arm and leg, light–headed and leaking precious blood he managed to haul open the huge oaken door.

Pausing on the threshold to look back over his shoulder, Lamenzo stumbled inside. His glance didn't mutate him into a pillar of salt. Through the scattering of streetlights they came, avengers silhouetted against a sky melting from purple to black. The four had become nine, their police uniforms as black as the cloth of night itself.

The door swung closed behind him, echoing hollowly in the vast chamber. Inside, the cool vault of the old church smelled of myrrh and spikenard and the slightly sweet aroma of burning votive candles. Father Joe knelt before the gray stone of the second altar, his balding salt and pepper head bowed in prayer.

The old priest didn't look around as Lamenzo staggered past the doorway between the Narthex and the Nave. He hobbled down the aisle, biting his tongue against the flares of molten lead shooting up his leg each time he put his left foot to the floor. It might have taken him an hour to walk the aisle.

Had he made it, it might have taken him longer.

Under the wings of Christ, Carlos Lamenzo finally succumbed to the hateful fire that burned away inside him. Death won the race to be with him. Touched his face, its hand as soft and cold as liquid glass. Claws of molten steel raked across his heart.

Hearing the slow groan of the double doors swinging open he let out a shaky exhalation. His lungs didn't have the strength to draw fresh air into them. Delirious, leaning against the sanctuary railing, a silent prayer on his fevered lips, he realized it was his last breath; one drawn as a child killer.

Taste left him, and smell. Touch. Sight. He heard voices, Father Joe's and someone else's, then sound was gone, too.

Falling onto his knees before the throne of God, Carlos Lamenzo collapsed, his heart giving in to the inevitable, and passed away into the darkness, the black, to be judged for his sins...

HALF a dozen agile policemen had stormed into St. Malachy's, three more still coming up the steps behind them, before Father Joseph D'Angelo realized they were heavily armed. They spread out to cover both sides of the Narthex, taking up positions between pillars, the crackle of their radios eerie and threatening in the quiet church.

To his surprise, D'Angelo found himself facing down the muzzle of a standard issue service revolver.

"What in God's name is the meaning of this?" The old priest demanded, rising awkwardly to his feet. Then, seeing Lamenzo slumped on the clammy stone floor, he breathed: "Oh, Sweet Jesus, Mary Mother of God..."

One of the policemen spoke while another knelt over the young man's corpse, checking it needlessly for a pulse. The final officers fell into position around the body.

"No disrespect, Father, but that son of a bitch down there," he gestured with the barrel of his gun at the body on the floor, "Just pumped a fistful of lead into the owner of a delicatessen over on Randell. Killed him, a six–year–old girl plus one unknown."

"No, no...I can't...he couldn't...no..." The priest breathed, shaken.

"He could and did, Padre, and right now it's my job to make sure he's not about to get up and do the same to you."

"Jesus, Mary...he might have had his troubles, but he...he couldn't."

"He's dead," the fresh–faced officer leaning over Lamenzo pronounced, standing and reholstering his pistol as he moved away from the body. According to his plastic lapel badge his name was S. Lawson. He was a big, gangling youth, all elbows and angles.

"Christ on a fucking crutch," another of the nine moaned, J. Bogdanovich, then swallowed, remembering where he was.

"Oh, Merciful Jesus..." D'Angelo rubbed a trembling hand across his eyes, they were damp with salty tears. "Can you help me move him?"

"Sorry, Padre. No can do."

"But he's..."

"Got to wait for forensics and the coroner, can't move him."

"This is a church, you can't just let him bleed all over the floor..."

"Sorry."

"Can't we at least cover him?"

"Certainly," Bill Stern said softly. "Do you have something? A sheet maybe? To act as a shroud?" He took a thick cigar from his pocket, didn't light it as he slipped it between his lips.

"Yes," D'Angelo said numbly.

Stern looked genuinely pained. "I'm sorry you had to see this, Padre, sincerely. If it could have happened any other way...but he ran here, like you could save him...would you mind fetching that sheet? I think the sooner he's covered up, the better, all things considered."

"Yes, yes..." D'Angelo said, shamed by the look of sympathy and understanding the officer gave him. "What kind of a world is it we live in, Officer? Can you tell me that? What kind of a world...?"

He turned his back and walked away, returning with the spare altar cloth. "In nomine Patris et Filia et Spiritus Sancti," whispered the priest, lowering the vestment. "Amen."

Lamenzo's sightless eyes were covered by the white linen. Flowers of red blossomed like the eyeholes in a Halloween lantern on the flawless cloth, one above the arm, two over the left leg. D'Angelo turned away, not bothering to hide his obvious anguish. "Well, I can't pretend that I like standing here like some vulture, gentlemen. If you don't mind, I've got a service to prepare."

"Not tonight, Padre." Bill Stern said, shaking his head. "I'm gonna have to insist you allow us to secure the church and that means no one comes in until the coroner's been. Standard operating procedure, I'm afraid. However, if you want to retire somewhere, by all means. The situation's well in hand. He isn't gonna cause us any more problems, so it's just a case of waiting now. If we have any problems we can't handle, we'll call for you."

"I suppose I am getting old and cynical, Officer, but I am becoming more than a little skeptical so far as miracles are concerned." The priest replied, looking again at the covered corpse, and back to the guns. "I'm sure he, may God bless his eternal soul, won't be giving you any problems." Crossing himself instinctively and genuflecting before the altar, the old priest bustled towards the sacristy door, very nearly missing the first miracle in St. Malachy's long history...

Reeek!

In the darkened chamber of St. Malachy's, where Carlos Lamenzo's body lay on the floor, a sound, as alien as straining metal, echoed.

Reeek!

Both Seth Lawson and Al Culpepper heard it, whatever it was. It wasn't the only sound in the church; there were other noises, mainly voices, soft and low in relieved conversation.

"Guess we got him good, eh?"

"Yeah, guess so."

But there was that noise, straining in the darkness. *Reeek!*

Silence returned, the waiting voices hushed by some primeval instinct coded deep in the genes. Eyes looked furtively, tongues dry and burnt out by tension stuck to sandpaper palettes.

"Jesus, I wish it wasn't so goddamned dark in here..." Someone complained. Jackson Carlisle or Jay Bogdanovich. Gabriel Rush?

In the darkness feet shuffled uncomfortably.

Someone sniffed. Someone else coughed.

And then there was light.

All at once.

Lights.

Colors.

Above the altar.

Around the head of Jesus, his crown of thorns burst into flames of dancing color. "Sweet Jesus..." It was Al Culpepper's voice. He stared at the body of Christ as it melted through the spectrum of colors, flickering, casting its rapidly shifting shroud of light over the congregation of nine below. He stared at the face of Christ, only it wasn't the face of Christ he saw painted on the wooden statue, it was his own. He was weeping tears of red, the stigmata, hands, ankles and sides bleeding likewise, tears of blood.

From on high, he grinned at himself and winked, blood smearing the flaking blue paint of his glossy eyes.

Al Culpepper fell to his knees, clasping both hands together, praying, the half–dozen flames of the votive candles in their red glass containers bathing his face, and Christ's face, crimson.

Then they weren't his eyes.

He blinked.

This time he saw the face of Carlos Lamenzo, the man he'd put three of his own bullets into, the dead man under the altar sheet, the killer, then it was no face but red...

No Face smiled at Culpepper.

Reeek!

That sound again. He knew what it was now. No Face had jerked a hand free of the spike crucifying it, tearing a raw–edged black hole through the statue's wooden palm.

Reeek!

His other hand wrenched free of the horizontal beam, the nail still piercing the palm. He wrenched his feet free, too, then the crucified Son of God stepped down and drifted to the floor, his miraculous passage bathing the church in the glory of Red.

Bill Stern heard screams, desperate shrill voices, men, women, pitched high and low, shrieking like a whirlpool of pain, the forlorn sound of death, rising and falling but always the cacophony of terror drowning out the exhaltations of frightened voices.

Al Culpepper had his hands over his ears.

It was a miracle the magnificent stained glass window of Jesus and St. Malachy didn't shatter.

Culpepper drew his pistol, holding it at waist height. It was all he could do to keep his hand from shaking. Maybe it was the work of the noise, the voices, he couldn't tell, but the shroud covering the dead man had been shucked off and lay discarded in a heap on the floor.

No Face took a step closer, reaching out.

Culpepper's heart was racing wildly out of control, and though he might, he couldn't believe that what he...what they all...saw was some kind of hysterical delusion.

Then, as abruptly as it had begun, the screaming ceased. The myriad other noises lying beneath the screams, noises they couldn't hear, disappeared with it.

Gradually, color by color, the erratic pulsing of lights faded from the gaudy carnival lightshow. Soon only a halo of red remained around the iridescent body of No Face, painting its gory pallet over the scene.

Inside, Al Culpepper felt some, claws of glass, rake over his heart, freezing it.

He was sure he was going to die.

He'd never been so sure of anything in his life.

He was right.

No Face stopped in front of him. It had his eyes again. His face.

Death reached out with a single finger. Touched him, slipping through the coarse blue weave of his shirt, burning through his chest, wriggling between third and forth rib, touching the smooth outside wall of his heart. Stilling it.

Then withdrew.

Oblivion swelled up to overwhelm Al Culpepper, blackness shivering through his bones, eating at the marrow until he fell the rest of the way to the floor, into the waiting arms of death.

Seth Lawson bolted for the sacristy, stumbling and weaving. The big, gangling youth seemed to be composed of long legs and arms of jelly, all elbows and knees. Retching sounds came from his throat as he struggled with the closed door.

Jay Bogdanovich stumbled a step back but couldn't take his eyes off the bloody red Jesus as it knelt over the body of Lamenzo. Frostlike ribbons of red ice were growing everywhere, spreading over every surface like a film of glass. The statue of Christ appeared to be weeping.

For the love of God...Bogdanovich's mind wailed as the statue laid aside its crown of glassy thorns...glass? They were wooden...and leaned down until his lips touched those of Lamenzo's, kissing the twin strips of bluish flesh and breathing life back into the lifeless body...

I'M dead, Lamenzo thought. The first thought of his new life. Tasting the dank breath of the wooden Jesus seeping down his throat, tasting the dry dead strips of varnished wood clamped over his own lips, the rancid tang of the air being forced into his lungs.

No, I'm not...

The wooden mouth went away, then came back, its touch glass. Breathed another rancid lungful of life into him.

Went away again.

He coughed and gagged on a mouthful of clean air. Normal air had never tasted so good.

He was alive again.

He opened his eyes.

He was lying on his back just beyond the sanctuary railing in St. Malachy's. Faces were looking at him, expressions a mixture of fear and amazement. Eight standing, one kneeling, one sprawled out on the floor much like he was...

Mostly fear.

He looked around, saw the guns leveled at him.

Why? He thought, and remembered...

Rosie Bossman.

He started to rise, drawing his unsteady legs under him.

Seeing him rise, the nine men gathered in the church fired. He heard the bark of bullets coming his way, then they struck him: upper thigh, groin, abdomen, cheek, spleen, lungs, heart, and arm. He felt them push him and twist him into a capering fool, but continued to haul himself erect. Someone fired again, bringing a second volley of fire. Two shots took him in the chest, one ploughed through his temple, another into his leg, four went wide.

"Look at me," he heard the kneeling figure say as it drew itself erect and reached out to take him by the hand. The hand around his felt as cold and heartless as an ocean of glass. "A life for a life...I've waited a long time. Do you want to live?"

"Do I want to?" he asked, a slight irritation in his throat and temple, from the bullet wounds. "Yes..."

"Good, come then..." His own personal Jesus reached into him, slipped into him, opened him like a book of bones and blood, occupied him, made him live and breathe...

Father Joseph D'Angelo, drawn by the riot of sounds, stood in the open sacristy doorway, clutching his faith in trembling hands. He could not believe, would not believe, the drama laid out before him. Though he saw the corpse reach out, its dirty fingernail smouldering as it bit deeply, burned, into the left cheek of an Indian officer. Though he saw the stained glass window of Jesus and St. Malachy melt around the thing that had once been a statue of The Son of God just as it had once been the dead body of a child killer lying on the cold stone of the church floor, though he saw the discolored patch of wall above the altar so recently vacated, though he saw the fallen body of Lieutenant Al Culpepper, and though Seth Lawson babbled in his ear, he could not believe.

In the window only a gaping hole remained, its shape that of Jesus Christ Our Lord in benediction. It was a hole plenty large enough for a body to escape through.

But he was dead...

BILL Stern was the first to speak.

"I don't know about you, but I sure as hell ain't saying I saw what I just saw…It didn't happen."

A few heads nodded as others agreed with him.

Silence for a moment, occupied by the aromas of spikenard, myrrh and cordite.

"What about Al?" D'Angelo didn't recognise the speaker.

"We say that fucker put a bullet in him, Jackson, easy as that."

"They'll know."

"Soon fix that," Bill Stern said, bringing his pistol up and aiming it at Al Culpepper's head. He pulled the trigger. "There. Now, what say we just tell them the bastard got away and forget all about it, huh?"

thirty three

He stopped reading and slipped the yellowed cutting back into his pocket.

And that was his story, The Trinity Killer, in his last breath a child killer, the lowest of the low, Carlos Lamenzo found life, breath, sanctuary in the arms of a God he never believed in.

Father Joe was gone and the truth was spreading thinner. He could smell them in the city, smell their guns, the air back to their bullets. Lawson was dead, and Bogdanovich. The others, the women, were just window dressing, to drag the eyes from the truth. Was he in their dreams? The men who had killed him? He hoped he was, hoped every time they closed their eyes they saw him rise again. He wanted to live in their dreams as much as they lived in his.

He wanted them to know they were spiritually if not physically dead.

Soon, he would look for the others.

Soon.

Maybe today, maybe not. Either way, he couldn't let the day end without tears.

He watched the woman pass, sniffed, could smell the dark–skinned cop on her, smiled to himself, a dead smile, then followed her.

"Sweet Ashley, save the last dance for me."

His cold laugh shivered through the glassy sky.

HE was tired. So very, very tired.

And he had good right to be. Most of the previous three nights had been wasted on fruitless searches through Brighton Beach and Oriental, and now, with the sun setting on another day he found himself moving out into the great wide open again, naked in a wilderness of concrete thieves. And that feeling of nakedness always left him vulnerable.

He looked down at the smudged headline again: Nik Lomas' name beneath: "Trinity Claims His Tenth." He felt a warm tingling sensation crawl up the length of his arms, almost as if some miniature farmer was ploughing shallow furrows of delight through the wiry tangle of his steely gray body hair.

He was The Watcher now. Back at the doors of St. Malachy's. Waiting.

He still felt bad about having to rush the priest. As it was, he had done a sloppy job of it; he'd only just finished the cutting, hadn't had time to run the stake through his heart to finish the dance of death he'd begun thanks to the interfering old bag and her damn wake–up call.

He rolled down the window, letting the cigar smoke leak out into the foggy evening, and leaned across the backseat to check on his tool bag again. Everything was there, as he had known it would be.

Smiling, he lifted out the sharpened piece of wood he was saving for The Father of All Things Bad with his crown of glass thorns, and tested its point on the pad of his index finger. A dewy drop of red welled up on the tip of the pudgy digit and started to congeal.

I haven't forgotten, he thought. I can still see your face, Lamenzo. I can still see your face...

Leaning his head out through the open window, The Watcher shouted: "Here I come, ready or not," as if it were some macabre game of hide and seek he was playing with the Devil. He gunned the car's idling engine.

thirty five

"Ashley," he tasted her name on his tongue as he chased her glittering halo.

The dance led him from street to backstreet, backstreet to alleyway to highway, across bridges, through tunnels and back again, The Trinity Killer sniffing out the woman's winding trail like some relentless bloodhound. And on her, heavy on her sweating skin, the stink of the cop.

Someone had sprayed "Snoop Doggy Dog" on the pavement beside "Notorious B.I.G." He ran over them, pushed passed a few milling people with downcast eyes set in odd faces. Faces that pushed desperately against the flimsy curtain of fog as if they were struggling against the taut stretch of cellophane. Sucking hard, struggling for lungfuls of unbreathable air. Their eyes would be dragged up and forced to look his way as he ghosted across their vision, and they would look, but they wouldn't see.

He felt the need of that thing inside him, the hunger, the barely audible whisper inside his head, goading him on.

"Soon," he soothed. "Just a little patience, my angel."

Lamenzo looked at the door that closed him off from his cornered quarry. Stark grained, designed to keep people out. On the side wall a panel of names paralleled a double row of buttons. Beneath the buttons a wire—meshed intercom system was set up. He ran a finger over the list of names, getting a feel for their individual colors, stopping on the fifth one, apartment 5a. The only one with the distinctive green—yellow combination of auras surrounding it.

He read the name plate.

"Ashley Powell."

And smiled as he pressed the button.

NIGHT was falling, New York City opening its foggy heart to the darkness.

Gabriel traced the curve of the scar on his left cheek, where the Trinity Killer's burning finger had marked him so cruelly. His eyes were a cried–out red in the rearview mirror. How many times? He asked the small photograph of Francesca half–tucked into the sunvisor. How many times am I going to cry over you?

He pushed the sunvisor back up. A menagerie of cars slipped by, picking up speed as they merged with the fast flowing traffic of the expressway. An artery in the city's motorway of veins, pumping vital blood into the coldly commercial heart.

Gabriel gently swung the Black Hawk back into the traffic, turning onto West 114th beneath the swaying citrus pines at the entrance of the Columbia campus, took a left and eased carefully onto a well–lit stretch of Broadway. He offered a thirty–foot tall David Letterman a wry smile as he rolled by the Ed Sullivan Theater.

Before him, the distinct brake lights of a yellow cab glared briefly. Behind him, the Empire State Building added its own heavy pall to the already gloomy city. People shuffled aimlessly about, wasting their aimless lives, crossing and re–crossing at the blinking lights, and ducking into and out of closing stores as they chased after rack after rack of needless bargains.

His foot on the brake, Gabriel eased out around the flashing tail lights of a double–parked Camero, changed down and sat in behind the dull gleam of an old Ford's lights.

On the radio a gravelly voice spliced Tori Amos into Joan Osborne into Lou Reed's Perfect Day. Gabriel leaned across to pluck the now heated lighter from the dashboard, lit the straggly licorice paper roll–up dangling between his lips and killed the singer. Alone. Only the sounds of the cars, the streets. A dull monotony of beats and rhythms.

Ashley's apartment was on the corner of Prospect and Vine, overlooking the red brick gargoyles of the Magdelena Chapel with their hunched backs and leprous eyes blind to the comings and goings of the underlife crawling about on the streets below. The streets around Prospect all looked the same. He pulled in behind a parked station wagon, crimping the tires against the sidewalk and pushing down on the hand brake.

Gripped the steering wheel hard, knuckles whitening as his fingers clenched.

Outside the five–story apartment block the fog had thickened so much so Gabriel found himself staring at the glowing tip of the cigarette, unable to see the Studebaker's stretched hood beyond it. A siren in the distance seemed to be calling out to him. Ambulance or squad car.

He sat and smoked, concentrating on nothing but inhaling the smoke, trying to taste the tar as it settled in his lungs.

The cigarette dwindled and the thoughts came slipping back like thieves of sanity. Hungry little beggars with dirty fingernails and blackened teeth

Leaning down, the ugly muzzle of Bill Stern's gun resting against Culpepper's forehead, black eye against the bruise and then the blood red rose flowering in the wake of the dead trigger...one shot opening a world of lies behind the miracle...sweet deceits and black lies... in a world of colored glass...

that claw and bite away on the thin wall between madness and the miraculous, tearing back the skin of the everyday to expose these raw wounds that cut deeply into his bruised psyche. The magic that shouldn't, couldn't, be real.

Gabriel turned the gold ring on his wedding finger, pulling it unconsciously towards the first knuckle as if taking it off. It wasn't coming off, not so long as her name was still inscribed inside the band: Francesca 2/24/1994.

He sank back into the driver's seat, his gaze drifting along the rows of dirty windows hiding dirty lives; living each one of those dirty lives in a few seconds, tasting the sickness behind the glass facade, and able to do so because somehow, somewhere, he'd stopped caring about them and slipped into the past. He knew, deep down where it mattered, he didn't love her, didn't love Ashley the way he'd loved Frankie, and that he wouldn't, couldn't, love her that way. Just couldn't.

He wondered what she was doing up there, wondered how he could tell her he doesn't love her? What words could he use to say goodbye to the rest of his life?

He reached inside the glove box for the makings of another cigarette. Remembered watching Francesca sleep. It didn't feel like that long ago. That long since watching her sleep had been his secret. His way of quietly thanking God. That was in the beginning of his life, when she was this porcelain miracle that walked fresh into his world, before Sam, before...and this, this was the end. Sitting there hurt.

It wasn't like that with Ashley. He didn't find himself looking at her face, falling into it, the way he had with Frankie.

But how long can you keep making love with your ghosts?

ASHLEY had just stepped into the shower when the buzzer intruded.

"Just bloody typical," she muttered to herself, wrapping a damp towel around her middle and stepping out. Stretching, she shivered and reached back in to shut off the stream of water.

The buzzer sounded again.

"I'm coming, I'm coming," she shouted, knowing whoever it was downstairs couldn't hear her anyway. Sliding the glass shower door closed, she padded out into the passage, her feet puddling sodden footprints on the carpet, the contrast of air from the bathroom to the kitchen bringing goosebumps to her patches of exposed skin. "Hello?" she said into the intercom's fake phone, brushing a strand of wet hair out of her face.

"Miss Powell?" a voice asked.

"Yes," she answered.

"Lamenzo's florists, Ma'am. Got a bouquet for you."

"Flowers?" she said, thinking out loud. "Bring them up." Shaking her head, she pressed the door release and looked around for her purse to tip the delivery boy. "Oh, Gabe, you sweet, sweet fool..."

THE Trinity Killer smiled at his reflection in the glass.

"Positively angelic," he said, and opened the door. "Like taking candy from a baby."

The foyer was a long, thin, high–ceilinged tunnel tiled with chipped alabaster and bordered on one side by a thick mahogany–stained balustrade that twisted around to crown the first flight. A strip of worn carpeting ran a line of emerald through the center of the tunnel, edged on both sides by strips of polished green linoleum.

"Yes, yes," he said, rounding the first flight of stairs and starting up the second, talking to the feeling inside him, the hunger. The second riser groaned under his weight. Up, up, and up again. The door to apartment 5A was the first of three on the landing. Behind him, the floor danced with a brittle glass–frost.

Something red ran, washed into his eye, staining the world the color of blood. He touched his forehead, felt the weeping wounds left by the crown of glass thorns. Strands of glittering light wove a hypnotic ballet around his ankles, twisting to the rhythm of silent belly dancers. He felt the touch of glass against his skin, burrowing a bloody passage into his ankle, grating against the calcine bone and cutting upwards, slicing through ligaments like some sort of coiled worm crawling through the dead skin of a roadkill, moving up, towards his gut. His skin rippled, the only outward sign of the glass's advance.

Another shard of blood red glass hooked into the cut in his torn jeans, coiled around his leg, freezing like a second skin of ice around the tense muscle, feeding a bloody red malevolence into his dead body.

Lamenzo threw back his head and tasted the air in back of his mouth, brimstone eyes wide with fire. Sand trails of sweat trickled down the crystalline sheen of his spine.

Downstairs, a door closed.

thirty nine

THE foyer reeked. Dead man's curls of sunfaded wallpaper peeled away from the wall. Stained yellow.

Gabriel Rush let the door swing closed and sniffed. Piss, probably a stray's. He started up the stairs thinking his way through another way to say what he had to say. Without even thinking about it, he stepped over the broken riser. The smell grew stronger the higher he climbed. Rounding onto the fifth–floor landing the fetid mess of odors could have masked the not–so–subtle perfume of an exhumation.

Taking a deep breath, he knocked on Ashley's door, the biggest part of him not wanting her to answer.

Behind him someone sniffed, an ugly wet sound, followed by a hacking cough. Instinctively, Gabriel stiffened, one hand moving of its own accord for the cold comfort of his gun as his mind picked a path through the minefield of bad scenarios tripping through his mind. He stopped himself from thinking about it and turned slowly.

There was a wretched figure hunched uncomfortably on the staircase, elbows on knees, holding his head in callused hands. Gabriel's hand drifted back to his side. Junkie, he thought, dismissively. Speedfreak...a second, uglier thought that began to blossom into a fast–wilting flower as the derelict looked up.

The man coughed again, a ragged abrasion of a sound. A bubble of caked phlegm dribbled down over the crest of his top lip and into his quivering mouth. The deadbeat's tongue licked out to lap it up.

Sickened, Gabriel turned away, but not before the wino's brimstone and winter eyes locked with his own. The eyes were sickly, veined with a turgid parody of Gabriel's cried–out tears. The eyelids fluttered closed, open, the wino staring through the windows into his damaged soul. Raking through his memories. Sifting the wreckage of his life for salvage.

Smiling sadly, the deadbeat licked at his spittle–flecked lips and lifted a jerky finger to his left cheek to trace the line of Gabriel's scar. Traced a slow, shaky circle around its length.

A black kind of understanding, like a lover's hand, stroked a line down the ridges of chest, cupping with cold certainty around

Gabriel's shrinking testicles. "Sacred Mother of the Blue Skies," Gabriel breathed, his voice betraying his clenched teeth in its need to be heard. He was unable to look away. Lamenzo looked bad, greasy coils of hair hanging in his eyes, skin desiccating beneath some kind of facial alapecia. Decaying, he thought, curiously distanced from reality. He's decaying, bit by bit. Cold air blew in from somewhere. He felt empty, gutted and soulless under the stare of The Trinity Killer. Couldn't bring his eyes away.

Cold heat flared in his chest, a lethal paradox that scoured like steel wool against the inside of his ribcage. Gone as quickly as it came. Nothing more than the ghost of a feeling left for dead in his chest. He was being drained somehow, he knew it, but knowing didn't mean he knew how to stop it. The murderer's chill caressed the fine hairs on the nape of his neck, chasing a shiver the down the ladder of his spine.

Face to face with this incarnation of Death, he felt a sudden powerful surge of terrified exhilaration. His vision filled with a dizzying colorshow, a Rorschach collage of yellow and blue and white, drowned finally by this all consuming red.

Just when it seemed the sensation would last for whatever was left of forever, he felt the miracle begin to fade; flecks of reality began to slither between the slipping curtain of color, spreading and blending to paint a whole. Gabriel blinked with eyelids that felt like raw foreskin and his Manhattan reality burned back to life all around him.

He felt the cold hand of fear close around his churning stomach, fingers curling, clenching, squeezing.

The Trinity Killer rose slowly, a hand clasping the wooden balustrade. He moved as if he was in mounting pain, the first bead of blood breaking on his forehead, bleeding his stigmata even as he smiled at Gabriel. "I can smell you, Little Indian Man. I can smell you like piss on the wind..." He reached out, a stop–motion slash as his burning finger slipped across Gabriel's left cheek, copying the first scar with a shallow cut. Blood ran through the stubble of Gabriel's cheek as Lamenzo touched the bloody finger to his lips and kissed it. "You're marked. I know you. I see you in my dreams." He blew the kiss back at Rush. "And you see me in yours...I know you do."

The first blood mingled with more cuts where each glass thorn had made its mark, where it had bitten deeply into the dead man's forehead. Tears of suffering cried above eyes too hard to care. Lamenzo lurched forward, left leg buckling then locking. His hand closed around Rush's throat, each fingernail a fragile claw as brittle and sharp as a slither of glass.

"I can see it in your memories, right beside." The killer's face tilted, as if hearing a whisper carried along by the creeping draft. Came back down smiling. "Oh, we're the same, you and me. We're the same."

"No. We're not the same."

"Yes. Yes we are." The killer crooned, the words tickling him. "We both kill children, but at least I never claimed to love my dead girl. Not like you."

Lamenzo slammed him back into the wall without releasing his grip, the dead man's glass fingernails raking ragged furrows into Gabriel's throat as he fell backwards.

The killer stepped back, made a gesture with hand and mouth, as if blowing out a light.

A life.

The whisper of death so soft between his fingers. "Soon," Lamenzo promised. "Soon, we do the dance for real and you join your dead son. Soon. It's a promise from me to you."

The shallow cuts burned. Something in them, a sickness left to fester beneath his skin, like dirt from those fingernails. Gabriel's head rocked back as if the strings supporting it on his neck had been cut. He twisted away from the corpse's touch and reeled sideways, slamming into the wall. A feeble moan touching his lips even as he reached out to brace himself with trembling hands. Head down, he gagged twice, vomiting onto the pea green sea of polished linoleum.

The echo of laughter drifted ghostlike down the hallway, accompanied by the more solid sound of footsteps lurching away. When Gabriel looked up he was alone in the corridor and the world was tilting. Desperately, he banged on Ashley's door even as he collapsed.

ASHLEY stepped out of the damp towel, leaving it in a pink puddle on the floor, and into her too short floral summer robe. Chinese silks embroidered with flower–breathing serpents.

She took a long hard look at her reflection in the full–length mirror and saw a tall, tanned woman with shoulder–length blonde hair that danced on the curve of her supple shoulders and tangled through the silver chainlinks of her heart–shaped necklace. Neat curves like the city itself, full of sights and delights and places to tempt the imagination right beside places made quite simply for eager hands to explore. She planted her hands on her hips, the silks riding up, and gave herself a twirl.

"Not bad, girl. Not bad at all." She laughed at her dizzy reflection, the faintest hint of a smile lingering cynically on her lips as she brushed the strands of wet hair back over her ears. "Not perfect, but pretty damn close."

The flower–boy knocked on the door again. With one last look back at her reflection she went to answer. As she reached for the guardchain the flower–boy knocked again.

"All right, already," she shouted through the wood as she reached up for the catch to open the door.

Instead of flowers she was greeted by a shape–a slumped body–spilling into her hall. Once open, the door refused to close. The weight of the body was too much for her to hold back. The door simply pushed itself open again allowing the body to tumble in; its disjointed bones concertinaing as it slid to the floor.

One second.

Two.

Three, as her face began to pull into a mask of panic.

Four, as she began to see, to really see...

The yellow, vomit stained lips, the cuts and the blood and the vacant eyes of Gabriel Rush staring sightlessly at her ceiling.

A gurgling, desperate moan knotted in the confines of her suddenly raw throat, sandpapering against the folds of flesh as she lunged forward, helplessly trying to catch him even though he was down.

It was several minutes before she could stop shaking, certain she was seeing death laid bare in its simplest of forms. She stood there in the hall listening to her own panicked breathing, a gradual coldness settling on her chill–puckered skin, the forgotten pepper–splashes of shower water turning to ice in the cold air.

"Please God," she begged, not knowing which God she was meant to beg to, hers or his. Her head began to throb thickly, as though trapped under the ice, drowning in a bad dream. "Don't be dead. Please. Don't be dead." Putting two shaking fingers up against his throat Ashley checked for a pulse.

It was there.

Now she felt calmer, more able to think.

A tear she didn't want to cry ran a leisurely course down her cheek. She sniffed and rubbed at her eyes. Pulling her robe tight to her own throat, she said a silent *thank you* to whoever and tried to lift him.

Light struggled behind the blinds, slanting vague rays of moon and streetlight through the slatted chinks.

Unconscious, Gabriel's body was as good as a dead weight. Ashley closed her eyes, refusing to look for the bullet wound she knew was there somewhere, the gunshot stealing this last chance at happiness. Another minute slipped away. Two more. She looked back over shoulder, to the door of the bedroom. Inside her head the room became a sanctuary to the madness out here in the hall. A place where the light couldn't find them. The place they had to be.

She knelt and slid her arms under his, trying to lift him again but forced to settle on a rough man–handled carry–drag across the floor which was the best she could manage. She heaved him into the bedroom and finally up onto the bed.

Ashley hovered uncertainly, gritted her teeth and began to undress him, each layer of clothing coming off as if it were bandaged across flayed skin. He groaned once, the only suggestion that he was even alive. Done, Ashley folded his clothes and left them on the wicker bedside chair as she went through to the bathroom. She felt the chill of linoleum replace the soft brush of carpet beneath her feet with minute shocks of ice. Balancing on her toes, Ashley searched the drug cabinet for Tylenol, put two on her tongue and washed them down with a mouthful of cold water. Then, walking as gingerly as if the floor were littered with fans of razorblades she went back through to the bedroom.

Gabriel was still out cold but his breathing was shallow and regulated, relaxed and calm once again.

Not dead, thank you God, not dead.

She walked back through to the hall and picked up the phone, wondering who she could call. Daniel Mannelli's face surfaced and she put a call through to the Westwood Precinct.

The Italian lieutenant listened anxiously, interrupting as she told him how she'd found Gabriel. Had she checked for wounds? Was he bleeding badly? What kind of wound was it? Should he call the paramedics? Ashley smiled nervously, chewing on the soft flesh of her bottom lip when he promised to make his own housecall.

Putting the phone down, she walked back through to the bedroom. She stopped in the shadowy arch of the doorway, eyes compelled, unable to draw her gaze away from the bed and Gabriel's fretful slumber. A shiver scuttled down her spine. It reminded her of a mortuary slab, a single white sheet spread over a still body. She tried to kill the illusion but it was inside her head now and it wasn't going anywhere. She felt her teeth sharp inside her lip as she slipped out of her robe, the iron tang of her own blood on her tongue.

"Oh, for fuck's sake," she hissed, hovering, unsure, before lying down next to him, spooning him neatly so that shins, thighs, belly, and breasts were all one single point of contact between them. The sheets were cold, still mortuary sheets in her mind, but it didn't matter because he was there with her.

She was no longer alone.

She lay there perfectly still, almost afraid to move for fear of waking him.

BRENDON Ellery stared at the open door of locker 31.

The darkness hiding the empty drawer.

No shroud.

No body.

No Father Joseph D'Angelo. He'd tagged and bagged the dead priest himself after the autopsy and filed it away in locker 31. Ellery stood back, fingers tapping impatiently on the edge of the locker door, marshaling his thoughts into some sort of logical order. He'd bagged the body and finally closed the file on D'Angelo, he looked up at the plain clock face, ten hours ago, over a week since he'd first come downstairs to Hospital Hell. Since then he'd taken lunch, cut open a crack baby dead two weeks before birth from congestive heart failure and dissected a septuagenarian who'd O.D.'d on domestic bleach after his wife's last lethal stroke.

No signs of a break–in. Nothing else missing.

Well, it's not as if he just did the Resurrection Shuffle out of here under his own steam. Ellery's face twisted into an ugly little smile as he closed the door on his erstwhile Lazarus' bed. *That's one option that's not happening.* He checked the residents of the neighboring lockers. The only viable alternative left, accepting the facts that A) the dead weren't walking and B) he wasn't losing it, was body–snatching. The thought didn't shock him; it numbed him.

He was a man of the world, and had certainly heard of weirder things, especially in high profile cases...including hideously maimed corpses waking up the moment before the scalpel made its first incision, but they were always before the cutting got underway.

Turning his back on the bank of lockers, Ellery pushed through the swing doors and into the twin smells of disinfectant and ammonia, hospital smells. An empty gurney rested against the wall. His footsteps echoed as he headed back towards reception, tongue clicking against the roof of his mouth, lips curling into a genuine smile as his eyes fixed on the surveillance camera at the end of the corridor, its single black eye looking down from above the swing doors.

"Got you," he said softly, pushing through the second set of doors into reception.

Brendon Ellery took the phone from the wall–mount and jabbed out the number of an office in Westwood, waiting for someone to answer. Mannelli picked up the phone, making it his problem.

forty two

THE Watcher's Coupe pulled up at the entrance to a seedy looking motel complex, beside a hissing neon sign. The middle two tropical–colored bulbs had blown, so in the full dark the hoarding advertised something called Paradise, about as close as the mismatch of rising cones, supplicant chimneys and rows of empty rooms could claim to being paradise. A series of hand–painted white lines marked off parking spaces and a small half–panelled door, boarded up where the glass ought to have been, served as the entrance to the reception.

Around the forecourt, windows hung open, some missing sheets of glass in their metal frames; garbage bins overflowed with empty beer cans, pizza boxes and McDonald's wrappers; fallen rain pooled in oil–streaked rainbows and hungry squalling seagulls fought over rashers fallen from the bins. He watched their aggressive dance, angled the wheel and rolled the car into a vacant bay outside the reception.

"Now don't you be getting any ideas about going anywhere," he said to the dead body on the backseat. "I'll be right back."

He slammed the door and ran up the short ramp to the reception.

The unwashed aroma of weeks old sweat clung to the little room.

Behind a battered looking plywood desk, a wrinkled Spanish relic sat reading a yellowed copy of *The People's Friend*. Looking up as he closed the door, she lifted a pair of fragile horn–rimmed spectacles from her wrinkled nose and cracked him a rictus of greeting. "You want a room, no?" she asked in methodical Pidgin English.

"Yes," he nodded.

"Ah, good good. Be so kind…Twenty five dollars, yes…" she mumbled to herself, lifting down the key to chalet 21. "Over on far side, by big bins, coin slot for TV takes 50 cents only, hokay?"

"Fine." The Watcher smiled, fumbling with his wallet for the money. He laid the bills on the counter. Her hand snaked out and snatched them away.

"Sign. Sign." She said, pointing agitatedly at a space in what he took to be the register, then she turned back to her book.

THE room wasn't a palace, but it was clean. It looked cheap and it smelled awful.

"Not that you're going to be complaining about the smell," he said to his roommate's body, slumped spinelessly in a cabbage–patterned lounger. A bare bulb hung from a naked flex, throwing 60 watts of pearl across the small room. Under its glare, the dead priest wasn't looking too healthy. "Now, I think we need to sort out some house rules, don't you?"

He began unpacking groceries from a straining paper bag. Stuffed olives, anchovies, pasta, ravioli, basmati rice, eggs, milk, coffee, noodles, ketchup, chicken fillet. Air freshener. "No bringing girls back without asking first. No loud music. Personal hygiene's important. You're not smelling so good, if you don't mind me saying. One shower a day, and use soap. I get the bed, you get the couch."

He uncapped the air freshener and sprayed half a can of Winter Harmony into the air. Coughing, he opened one of the metal–framed windows. "Ah, now there, that's better isn't it."

He took a fat cigar from the tin in his coat pocket, peeling away the shrink–wrap. Bit off the leafy end and chewed tobacco before he lit it, drawing the petrol taste of his battered brass lighter deep into his lungs. Coughed a deep tubercular cough. Tapped the ash tip off on the carpet and fed 50 cents into the television.

"Now, what am I going to do with you?"

GABRIEL stirred and immediately groaned, feeling hot, bloody pain lance through his spinning head.

His first conscious thoughts were purely physical: hunger, thirst, the need to release the pressure building in his bladder.

The thud of a newspaper on the doormat, bringing its bad news. His mind turned inwards, trying to decipher the bewildering array of messages that whirled and spun their jig inside his head.

Pictures, as hazy as the room about him, swam across the fever dream hinterland of his gradually forming consciousness.

In one, a wino wearing a crown of glass thorns held a fingernail to his head and carved away the bone. In another, a woman, bathed in the heat and the sweat of the act, opened herself up for knives. Another, a bleached corpse bloodied with a scrawl of tattoos telling the murderer's story.

The flashflood of images rolled on, gathering momentum. "We're the same, you and me...we're the same..." A blow out. A car, too close to the white line, too close to the curb, weaving drunkenly across the road. Driver fighting for control. Running a red light. Up on the sidewalk, people falling away in every direction. On the asphalt, burning rubber, throwing himself clear as the car slides into the side of a petrol tanker, licking up into a hateful conflagration.

The images punched into his head in a series of hammer blows—breaking glass, the diesel stench, the flame, smoke, darkness, death.

And in there, in its heat: Sam and Frankie.

Unable to pull away from the wreckage, his spirit floated towards the buckled door, into the heart of the firestorm, ethereal hands burning as they struggled desperately to open it, ghost eyes streaming under the insidious biting of the smoke's teeth, knowing it was impossible, too little too late. The heat of the flame beating him back.

Through the glass he saw a young boy, blood matted in his hair, eyes opening to see his death all around him in the licks of fire and the choking gulf of smoke, to see his mother's body half–in, half–out of the car, diamonds of shattered windscreen and a spreading pool of blood beneath her too–white face.

Smoke blind, Gabriel screamed with his son's voice. To lose him now, again, when he was so close...

The same tears of loss were pouring from his smoke–stung eyes. He grappled with the buckled door, the metal stripping the flesh from his palms, burning him to the bone, but even in the dream the door wasn't opening. Crying for his dead son, Gabriel gave up on the door and struggled to drag the corpse of his wife from the blaze.

Her ruined face stared blindly at him, mouth falling open, head lolling. A bloody spider crawled out through the crack between her lips and scuttled around the curve of her neck. Another bloody leg twitched through the broken lips. Another spider. And another. Swelling out of Francesca's mouth, bloody legs of blood smeared spiders being born out of his wife's head, crawling over her cheeks, her eyes, her hair, and still more being born from between her lips.

Only they weren't her lips, beneath the bodies of bloody spiders her face melted into the thin lipped smile of a Latino angel with a face of finely carved glass.

"We're the same, you and me...we're the same..."

forty five

GABRIEL came out of the dream: sat bolt upright in bed, sweat clinging to his fevered skin, gasping for a breath that wouldn't come.

Beside him, Ashley shivered and pulled at the covers, bringing the sheet up under her chin.

He looked at her. Her heart beating against the mattress.

Looked at himself.

Somehow, she had contrived to sleep entwined with him, her legs wrapped around his, each time she moved her thigh brushing innocently against his penis. Angry, at himself as much as her, Gabriel wriggled free of her leg–embrace and swung himself out of their shared bed. His legs gave way under him as he remembered *"We're the same, you and me...we're the same..."*

"No we're not," Gabriel bit down on the pain, pressing his fingers into his temples in an attempt to blind the memory. Fighting back. "We're not the same..."

In the bed, Ashley stirred, rolled over and lost the edge of the sheet covering her. He looked down at her slumbering innocence as she rolled again, the flesh around her breast wrinkling up as she squashed it against the yielding mattress. Watched her pulse in the soft white curve. The fresh not–quite–morning chill had stiffened her nipple; darkening it to a husky brown around the puckered aureole.

But she's not Francesca, he caught himself thinking.

"No, she's not," he half–whispered as she drew her leg up, gradually exposing the darker triangle of hair, the edge of velvet between her silken thighs, and felt a hardness creep into his groin, slowly, teasing, stiffening. *She's Ash, and I was so close to throwing it all away...*

Before he could change his mind, Gabriel lowered himself back onto the bed and leaned in to kiss the nape of her naked back, tonguing the soft hollow just above the swell of her buttocks, forcing all thoughts of Francesca from his mind.

"Ash," he breathed, needing to hear her name. She stirred slightly, her delicious shiver tracing through his fingertips as he explored.

TOGETHER, they touched, tentatively at first, then with more assurance, fingers opening doors to pleasure, they tasted, tongues on the salt skins, drank with their eyes, ate with fingertips, the muscles of their bonded bodies merging into a single song.

The delicious shiver as he entered her, her legs wrapping, locking around his back, pulling him in, fingernails raking in, needing to feel him.

Moans, sighs then whimpers; a final scream–like sound.

Then, release.

She held him, head resting on her collarbone, eyes closed as she smoothed her fingers over the black bird painted on his shallow–breathing chest.

Together, holding each other, needing the intimacy and comfort of skin against skin, they passed the remains of dawn making gentle, leisurely love to the quiet harmony of waking birds.

Ashley Powell was a live–life–pretty–much–as–it–comes kind of woman, her life a perfectly balanced knife–edge between chaos and the abyss of order. Things had a way of getting done, but only when they absolutely had to be done. Her apartment was a perfect reflection of her character, cluttered, carefree with just a hint of playful sensuality beneath.

She packed as she lived. Quickly, bustling about the empty bedroom doing a passable imitation of a decapitated fowl, she pulled seemingly random garments out of the closet and jammed them into the battered overnight bag on the bed. The afterimages of their bodies were still burned into the crumpled sheets like the radiation shadows of holocaust victims.

Ashley fumbled with the top drawer of the dresser, grabbed a handful of lacy black and stuffed it in on top of the wrinkled edge of her only CK blouse. As an afterthought, she flattened the wrinkled surge of ripples away. She cast a quick glance back in the direction of the bathroom even though she could hear the primal tattoo of the shower water splashing down on the bathtub.

Okay, plenty of time, she told herself, digging through her make–up bag for a kohl eye–pencil. Her hand trembled ever so slightly as it drew a line around her watering right eye, the blunt pencil painting its shades of color in. She used a rubber band to put her hair up. Tried smiling at her mirror self from two or three angles with two or three different smiles, trying them on for size.

"Hey," Gabriel's sleep–filled voice called from the doorway. "Where're you off to in such a hurry?" His reflection was looking at the overfilled travel bag on the bed. He still looked like warmed–through shit, naked but for the damp–darkened towel wrapped around his waist. Red–rimmed eyes heavy with more tears smiled softly her way. More than anything, Ashley found herself wanting to throw her arms around Gabriel and hug him so fiercely he split through the middle. She turned around to face the real Gabriel, look him in the eye, and felt herself wanting (when had she last felt like this? *Too long ago* was the answer) to cry for him.

"Nowhere without you," the slight catch in her voice giving away more than she wanted to say. "Oh Gabe, I don't know. After last night...I don't want to be here for a while. I thought we could be alone for a while...somewhere..." she let it hang, wanting to say so much more about ghosts. About his ghosts. The two of them that lived in every building, on every street corner in Manhattan and The Bronx. She knew he knew and hated herself for nearly saying it. He'd earned the right to mourn, as a father and as a husband.

She blinked back tears of her own as she watched the emotions jostle for position behind his eyes, wished she could take back every word, every thought until he stepped out of the doorway, arms held wide for her to step in to.

"I know," he said softly, taking her in his arms, closing them around her. Gabriel brushed an errant curl back and touched his lips to the top of her head. "I think I might, you know..." He didn't say it, couldn't.

"Me too," she swallowed, feeling the strength of his body against hers and the slow track of her tears on her smiling cheeks.

While Gabriel packed the few bags into the trunk of the Black Hawk, Ashley slipped into the bathroom, taking the opportunity to rinse the mingled aromas of sweat and his sex from her skin, and luxuriated in the comforting warmth of the water pouring from the shower head. The dim light streaking in through the small hatch window grouped in tight clusters of brightness, like mottled freckles on the glass face of the shower door.

Showered, the faintest tang of Gabriel's scent still clung to her skin, acting as a reminder of their first night and morning spent coupled as lovers.

Toweling herself off, Ashley dressed in a tight pair of faded denims and a loose cotton blouse and locked up. As she closed the building door, she saw Gabriel sitting on the Studebaker's stretched hood, his eyes looking somewhere into the foggy distance.

"Penny for them," she called, coming down the steps.

If anything, the mist that had slowly descended on New York the day before seemed to be getting worse.

"Not worth it," Gabriel mumbled, slipping down off the hood, the last of his vision slipping away as his eyes drew in to focus on her.

IN two hours they climbed away from the heady sky-scrapers of glass and steel and the clammy street fogs, dipping in and out of pockets of smog before they hit the five–lane Interstate. Ashley reclined lazily in the passenger seat, the sun visor up, basking in the refracted rays of the midday sun.

They followed the serpentine trail of the 187 road-way, meandering through a bitter series of corners and diminishing rows of gray stone before rising over the Tappan Zee Bridge and moving out into the country, passed Wilkes–Barre and Scranton, leaving the crazy hubbub of city center roads further and further behind.

Gabriel watched Ashley through the rearview mirror as she stared through the dimpled pin–pricks of the roof–lining, eyes unfocussed. She'd hardly said a word since they'd cleared the Hudson. Watching her through the mirror it was obvious what was going on inside; the thoughts behind the eyes. She was afraid to ask about what had happened immediately before she'd opened the door on his unconscious body. They were the same thoughts (*we're the same, you and me...we're the same*) that had curled lazily through Gabriel's mind five times an hour since he'd woken, the ones he hadn't dared give voice to for fear of making them more substantial.

More real.

And they were eating her up, these thoughts, and still she was saying nothing.

So they drove in silence, passing into and out of Scranton before Ashley opened the glovebox on a few sun–bleached cassettes sheltered between a dirty chamois leather, the black flap of his shoulder holster and a box of tissues, half–hidden in the cool shadows, their lettered inlays faded beyond reading.

She picked one at random, pushed it into the player. The tiny screen was lit up by an insipid glow, a double row of squares pulsing like a heartbeat in rhythm with Leonard Cohen's end–of–the–world vocal.

"Happy happy, joy joy." Her first words for over an hour. Her last words for another hour.

Through the rearview mirror, Gabriel watched his battered old fedora slide between the speakers.

Near sundown, Gabriel turned off the Interstate and drove down into Smalltown USA, parking on the wide main street across from the ramshackle wooden form of Al Straker's General Store, in line with a neat row of jeeps, Toyota's and dusty old Ford's. The blinds were down and the awning was up. The sign on Straker's door said:

CLOSED FOR THE NIGHT
WHY DON'T Y'ALL COME BACK AND SEE US
IN THE MORNING

Much of the town looked like Straker's; box houses of slatted wooden frames squatting in the middle of small patches of Eden, bordered by blacktop. No sidewalks. No cars to talk of either. Not driving.

They went for dinner at Sal's Country Kitchen, choosing to sit out on the veranda and catch the last of the sun's failing rays. Beyond the rail the glitter of an old creek puddled, catching rainbows from the sky and throwing them out in hypnotic ever–decreasing circles of shifting color, the creek's watery sides lined with cypress and pines.

"Beautiful," Ashley breathed, her voice as slippery as the invisible fish bathing beneath the surface.

"Yeah," Gabriel agreed, thoughtfully. "And then some."

When the food arrived they were both pleasantly surprised. Sal, it seemed, had discovered the secret of the perfect pizza.

"So, what do you reckon?" he asked when they got back to the car. "Do we look for a cheap motel for the night, or do we go on?"

"What do you fancy? You're the one driving. It's going to be long past midnight when we land."

Gabriel shrugged his shoulders, working out a cramp before he'd even got in behind the wheel. "I could probably do with a break from the driving but otherwise either way suits me just fine."

"No problem then," Ashley grinned, holding out her hand. "Gimme the keys."

Hand around his jaw, Gabriel whistled out a short breath. "Don't know about that...the old girl's a bit on the sensitive side, needs plenty of T.L.C. just like her old man. You think you can handle that?"

"Just shut up and give me the keys."

"Whatever you say, honey bunny," and then to himself, "Anything for a quiet life."

"Treading on thin ice, Rush," she warned. "Very thin ice."

"Whatever you say."

"Okay, wise guy. Don't say you weren't warned."

Opening the side door and ducking into the passenger seat, Gabriel nodded thoughtfully. "Right, I think I'll shut up now."

"You do that," Ashley agreed, sliding the keys into the ignition and turning over the rest–cooled engine.

"Music?" he asked as she reversed out between the line of parked jeeps.

"Help yourself." It was the closest he was going to get to a yes.

There was a trap in the glovebox, a lure to hook him back to everything he was trying to forget; memories and music entwined like forever lovers. The haunting strains of Tears bringing back the sad, timeless feeling of watching the seasons fail while his mind ran back to the day everything in his old life died, moving him gently toward the tears of the title.

The song finished seconds before they rejoined the Interstate. Gabriel cut the next song short, rewinding the tape to play it through again.

Even concentrating on the darkened road and the tube–like tails of light streaming out before her to form an elaborate grid of gold and red, Ashley could feel the pain haunting him.

"Want to talk about it?" she asked as he rewound the tape again.

"Not much to talk about, really." Gabriel lied, fingers concentrating for him.

"Try me anyway. I'm a good listener."

"Maybe later," he said, giving himself up to the same army of ghosts again.

"Whenever you feel like talking," Ashley said softly, moving out to overtake a hulking Merry Maid 16–wheeler.

He was asleep by the time they passed the last exit for Utica, curled up in a tight fetal ball with his face pressed against the glass of the passenger door.

"Next stop paradise," she told his sleeping form, seeing the sign for Syracuse lit up in the distance, the soft voice of her words too quiet to be heard above the humming of the Black Hawk's rumbling engine.

Gabriel groaned and half–stirred.

Without the distraction of cars on the other side of the glass, and little else out there to hold her attention for more than a few seconds, Ashley felt the deadly caress of sleep creeping up on her. The regular monotony of passing alone through the dull puddles of sodium streetlight, soporific in itself, and the ebb and flow of Gabriel's breathing didn't help.

With the stars acting as token light–bearers in place of the sleeping sun, Ashley pulled in at one of the roadside cafes.

She had nearly overshot the turn, attracted at the last minute by a barbershop beacon that flashed OPEN irregularly; its slow–moving life, the shadow of a working waitress up against the window and the overriding need for a caffeine fix, calling out to her.

She left the engine idling so as not to wake Gabriel, and ran across the asphalt to a small, anonymous serving hatch. It was a pleasantly mild night.

"Coffee?" she asked a waitress and was rewarded a pasty faced nod. "Great. Make it strong. No milk, no sugar."

The waitress made a show of wrapping a well–chewed ribbon of gum around her painted nails. "Thirty–five cents," she muttered, replacing the balled–up piece of gum and chewing."

Ashley pulled a rumpled bill out of her tight hip–pocket and handed it over. "Keep the change."

The girl's face mellowed as she pocketed the sixty–five cents change, the stranger walking into and out of her life with a bubble of pink gum.

Gabriel hadn't so much as stirred.

As she sipped at the steam–wreathing liquid, Ashley reached across and, keeping the volume low, turned on the radio. The last few words of the midnight news bulletin before the intrusion of the station's tuneless jingle. She killed the noise, and opened the door again to throw the empty cup out through the crack.

They made Syracuse in good time, passing the city limits sign a little after 3 a.m.. Twenty minutes later, she took the Studebaker up onto the finely graveled path that crawled around the edge of a shimmering moonlit lake, the tires crunching on the stone chips covering the track. She eased the car to a stop beside a gatepost, a short way from a dark–shrouded hunter's cabin. A finger–thin sliver of moonlight reflected on the ripples of shallow water lapping against the shoreline.

Ashley leaned across to wake Gabriel. "We're here, Gabe," she whispered, shaking his shoulder gently until he groaned and opened his eyes. "We're here," she repeated, quietly, as he rubbed the sleep from his eyes and stretched.

A banked–up log fire crackled and spat in the grate, the glow of its flickering dance the only light; its smell, a heavy oaken musk, was a small slice of heaven.

Gabriel stretched, his shoulder sheened with the fragrant sweat of sex, his back stippled with beads of it like a cool beer bottle on a hot, dog day. "Feels good," he said, running his fingers through the unfastened tangle of his matted hair, savoring the warmth of the fire.

Beside him, Ashley murmured her contented agreement.

Ashley had laid a plaid blanket out before the unmade fire while Gabriel scavenged the woodpile for a few sturdy chunks of dried timber before rooting through the cupboards for the firelighters, coke and tinder to ignite the blaze.

Then together, on the blanket: at first neither one of them dared to so much as move for fear that the spell of perfection might shatter, leaving them alone again. To end that awkwardness Gabriel leaned forward and kissed the hollow of her bare neck, his tongue savoring her taste. His hands moved in gentle caress, fingers walking down the smooth ladder of her spine until they touched the rough edge of denim and began gently working loose the hem of her blouse, gathering in the folds of cotton and lifting.

Ashley's hands worked clumsily at undoing his belt, fingers fumbling.

It was like the first time for both of them; the first time they'd suffered the uncertainty of undressing, of laying themselves bare. Neither knew the other well enough to know what might come next, how they might respond to a certain touch, but they worked with a singularity of purpose born of need, two people who had found each other in the dark, shedding clothes like skin as the orange flames danced in the hearth, snapping and crackling with their tentative explorations, as the air around them filled with the heady perfume of their eventual lovemaking.

"No," Gabriel said, arching his back as he stretched. "It feels better than that." He reached out and prodded at the fire with a gnarled wooden poker, watching the logs shift uncomfortably under his inspection, the face of Carlos Lamenzo forming in his thoughts.

Ashley sat up, her fingers massaging the knots out of his tight shoulders. Waiting for him to say what was weighing on him so heavily.

"I've felt like running away before," he said without turning his gaze from the sporadic dance of the flames. Her hands shifted, kneading the bunched muscle around his neck.

"Everyone thinks about running away some time, Gabe. It's not a crime. The thing is, you stayed."

We're the same, you and me...we're the same...

Gabriel moved his hands up to cup Ashley's as they worked on his spirit. "I should be out there looking for him. I don't think I could forgive myself if someone else died because I wasn't there to stop him."

"Relax," she soothed, her hands moving back across his shoulders and down his back, touching, rubbing, probing and pushing gently. Always gently. "You're a bundle of knots, Gabriel. You're going to have to relax. Forget about the real world. It doesn't exist anymore, okay?"

Gabriel sighed. It felt good. Her practiced hands roaming his skin, working the clusters of stubborn muscles, but he couldn't forget about the real world. Lamenzo was out there, possible or impossible, it didn't matter. The truth mocked everything he believed in. All he had, all he could trust, his own eyes. *We're the same, you and me...* The dead man's voice reared in his ear.

Things were happening, a long way from taking photographs and tracking down bail jumpers, things were happening inside and outside and Bill Stern was wrong, there was still space in this brave new world for the Spirit Magic of the older one. He'd seen Lamenzo go down beneath the twisted waltz of their guns.

"Ash?"

"Yes, Gabe?"

"I've got something kind of important to tell you." He shifted his weight onto one elbow, bottom lip caught between teeth as he looked her in the eye.

"Better tell me then." She couldn't keep the smile out of her eyes, his face was so serious. "Not an alien from Z'bob 3 this time?"

"I think I love you," he said simply, shrugging away the embarrassment with a sheepish smile. "I mean with all this other stuff, I don't know...I just feel it here." He tapped his heart.

Without saying a word, Ashley stood, holding out her hand for him to take. She led him to the door.

"Where are we going?" he asked, eyes following the patterns of flexing muscle and the graceful motion of her body, and the glitter of her oiled skin in the shifting light. Turning, Ashley smiled, while her hands worked the deadbolt free.

"For a swim."

"A swim? As in in the lake? Now? Are you crazy?" He cupped a protective hand around his testicles. "It'd ruin me."

Ashley laughed. "Come on fishboy, it'll be good for you." She opened the door and slipped out into the dark night, bare footsteps echoing her run down to the water's edge.

The cold night air closed around Gabriel's body like an icy hand. He ran after her, watching her flit through the moonlight, bare feet dancing across the wide bole of the cinder track, carrying her ever closer to the water. Ragged chips of gravel dug into his feet. Her laughter, the distant call of a whippoorwill, the gentle rush of water lapping against the shoreline and then the splash of Ashley diving into the black expanse echoed back to him. Not even the sound of a car, he thought, realizing the truth of silence as he reached the bank.

"How's the water?"

"Fucking freezing...you coming in?" She submerged, letting the water close over her head until her hair spread out like a finely feathered peacock's tail, catching and twisting the moonbeams with their subtle ripple.

The chill wind puckered his skin. Shivering, Gabriel hugged himself and turned away from the lake. Behind him, Ashley shot from the murky depths, gasping as the frigid air closed around her naked body like a second, crystal skin. A great spume of water fountained from her mouth.

"I hope you're going to warm me up," she shouted, splashing her way out of the water.

Gabriel turned and blew her a kiss. "Maybe," he called. "But then again, maybe not."

"Bastard," she laughed and raced him back to the fire.

FINGERS tapped softly against the veil of his dream.

And another sound: like the tumbling of empty cans down a wet gutter. A figure, dark, ragged and faceless under the dull red cast of the blood moon shuffled towards his bed, palsied limbs twitching and jerking as they reached for him. He lay still, eyes closed against the horror in the vain hope it would pass by him.

A smell came to him, a rancid, long–since–turned smell.

A floorboard creaked as the pressure on it shifted.

He felt his muscles tightening, the small hairs on his scalp prickling beneath the electricity of fear.

Touches against his skin, by turn dry, cold, hard, wet.

Another sound, a deflating sigh.

He wanted to open his eyes, to look at the dead man in the chair, but what if…what if…what if he wasn't in the chair anymore? What if it was the dead man's breath he felt on his cheek, the dead man leaning over him like his mother, fingertips brushing the hair from his forehead?

His eyes flickered, fighting the instinct that begged them to stay closed, and opened.

A face, dead–eyed and blanched pale, smiled down at him.

And swooped…

…The Watcher threw himself backwards, fetching the back of his head against the metal bedstead, hands up instinctively to ward off the nightmarish fangs of the dead priest. He could feel his heart in his throat, beating wildly on a collision course with the mortuary slab.

"Oh, Jesus…oh, Jesus…"

Father Joe was still propped in the chair as dead as he had been five hours ago.

The Watcher flinched as the dead man's hungry face retreated back into his subconscious, the last vestiges of the nightmare hanging over him. He climbed out of bed, walked over to the dead priest propped in his cabbage–patterned lounger, and beat the pallid leer off his face with the full force of his fists.

AGAIN the nightmare awakened him.

He lay on his back in the dark while an errant shutter banged against the window frame. It was the same dream, where he dreamed he was a dead man who dreamed he was alive. In that tangled web of dreams, fragments of memories buzzed like angry fireflies: the dull sepia–toned faces of his children, alive, then dead, then alive again; his mother, father, mother, father, mother...Liz, trapped in a distant photograph. And Father Joseph D'Angelo held the photo album of his life, turning the pages.

When you are ready, the dead man seemed to say, fleshless lips not so much as twitching.

He felt the proximity of death and screamed, thrashing wildly, fighting it, flailing, failing, fading.

D'Angelo's red eyes faded to brimstone. A dead finger touched the flesh of his eye.

Soon...soon...a threat—no, a promise.

Something scampered over his bare feet in the darkness, and this time The Watcher did not stop screaming, screaming over and over again.

"GABE?"

The darkness split into diamonds, showering such light that he imagined the sun would fall. For long moments he was a mote in the heart of the furnace, then, gradually, the fire subsided and his world drifted back into its place around him.

A face.

Through the aureole of light.

A divine smile, meant for him and him alone.

"Gabe?"

The light faded further, the fingers of his dream fading. Raindrops on the window. He saw tears glistening in Ashley's eyes, saw her lips tremble as she made another attempt to speak, give up, and show her love in a more direct way. She leaned forward and hugged him as tight as she dared.

Gabriel held her close until her tears had run their course, asked no questions. As gently as he could, he broke the contact between them, his hands on her shoulders easing her away until he could look into her bleary eyes. "It's all right, Ash," he soothed, smoothing away a sleep–matted bang of hair and kissing her forehead tenderly. "Everything's all right."

She tried to speak. "I thought...oh dear God I thought you were gone..."

"Shhh, honey. I ain't going nowhere without you."

She stared at him, through him, as if he were a ghost, then began to weep again, her whole body raking with the sobs. "You looked...you looked like you were dead...I felt so sure I'd reach across and you'd be cold...Gabe, I was so frightened..."

He wanted to say: I'm sorry, Ash. I'm so sorry...I don't know what's happening, but I do know it's bad, whatever it is...I'm scared...I can feel him out there getting closer all the time and I don't know what to do, how to fight him...

Instead, rather awkwardly, he said, "Just scary monsters. How about pancakes for breakfast?"

Ashley smiled. Her face still looked pinched and pulled with ache, but it was a smile.

"Maple syrup?"

"You betcha, maple syrup, ice cream, the works. Nothing's too good for my baby," he said, taking her delicate, pale hand in his own leathery one, twining her fingers with his. He squeezed her hand and kissed her forehead again. "Some tough guy P.I. I make, huh?"

"The best," she agreed. "Now, how about those pancakes?"

THE morning brought rain.

Not the torrents of winter rain so typical of Syracuse, but a fine drizzle. The day moved on, growing grayer, and so, it seemed, did Gabriel's mood. Though Ashley made hourly attempts to coax him away from the stone he'd made his lakeside perch, he wouldn't move.

All she could do was stand by and watch. And watch and watch, helpless to prevent his fall. Surely dying was like this, she reasoned; losing precious moments and being unable to prevent their passing.

Yes; this was a kind of death.

The worst.

It was well into the last hour of Sunday, the moon scudding across the sky towards midnight, when Gabriel came in from the cold and unburdened himself.

Ashley was in the kitchen, readying a couple of mugs when he called through.

"You said you wanted to listen?" he mumbled, looking at the floor.

"Only if you wanted to talk," she said, joining him cross–legged on the floor.

"I want to, I guess."

He didn't move, didn't say anything. Just sat there, chin resting on his knees, watching the secret dance of the fire drawing to a close.

"I miss him you know..."

He was crying now, or trying very hard not to.

"I miss him so much."

Ashley slipped her arm around him, drawing him into a gentle embrace.

"It's not fair..."

"No, it never is."

"Why though? What did he do? He was only a child...three..." Gabriel swallowed, wiping his eyes with the back of his hand. "Why didn't I die? Why? WHY?"

"Gabe, don't talk like that, please." Ashley reached out to touch him, to soothe him, but her fingers fell hesitantly short.

THEY rolled into New York early on Monday morning, slipping off the I87 and skirting the still quiet of the city streets with their neat little gardens hemmed in by their neat little iron railings.

A murky haze had banked up city side of the Tappan Zee bridge, thin floss tendrils licking around the old Studebaker as it picked its path homewards.

The words had been said lightly, almost as a joke, but with too much honesty to be genuinely hollow. "How about making an honest woman out of me, Tonto?"

"I'm still married," Gabriel let his voice trail off. "In here." He tapped his chest, his heart. And Frankie was back with him, between them, with the sounds of horns and the rumble of engines announcing their return to the city.

Pulling up outside Ashley's apartment building, Gabriel killed the idling engine and climbed out. They walked arm in arm to the doorstep. He leaned over, placing a tentative kiss on Ashley's forehead; a kiss goodbye.

Ashley balanced on tiptoes, pressed her lips against his, tongue teasing a soft path across his teeth. Her taste, touch, smell, became a heavy cross of feelings. A weight. It had been so very, very long since he had felt this good about anything.

He backed off a step, looked at her. Held her eyes. Tried to smile. "There's something I've got to do. A ghost I've got to exorcise. It's been a long time due. I can't keep putting it off." It wasn't quite the truth. "It'll take a couple of days, but I'll be back. I promise. You look after yourself, kiddo."

"You too, Tonto," she said, sadness wearing her voice like a halo.

HE drove for hours, hours stretching into a day, a night, another day, leaving Ashley and Frankie far behind. The road and his soul. The song of the blacktop. The feel of it humming beneath the driving wheels. The driving was out of habit, his feet moved, braking and accelerating, his hands steered, changed up and down through the gears and indicated around corners. Weaving in and out of backed–up traffic, Gabriel drove, passing from mainstreet to highway and back, out into the country, along the rim of a lake.

He stopped to use a pay phone. To call Ashley. Just to hear the sound of her voice. Looking for some kind of reaffirmation in the real, the solid, the simple. Her machine picked up, bright and breezy: "Leave a message sugar–lips, and I'll get back to you. You know there's a beep coming…"

The same message twenty–four hours later. And again the next five times he called over the next three hours. He looked back the way he had come, three days of road between them and nothing he could do, not realistically. Looked on into the future, miles of road unwinding before him. Not knowing what to do, caught by indecision, Gabriel turned to the sky. He took the hunting knife from the glovebox and lay it on the white line dissecting the blacktop. Span it, looking for an arbitrary hand to give him an answer he could believe in. The blade glittered in the too–hot–to–be–refreshing sun, caught the light, made it dance silver as it rotated, slowing, wobbling before it stopped to point the way.

Montana.

He went back into the phone booth and tried Ashley's number one last time before sinking back into the driver's seat.

For a while, his right side was clear blue water and lake–bound boulders. Over the horizon, the sun's valiant attempt to hang on to the heavy, smothering layers of dull steel–gray cloud appeared to be a lost cause.

A sign up ahead indicated a change of routes for Montana. A small B–road.

The road behind him was empty. Gabriel veered off without indicating, passing between a canopy of dark trees. It was unnerving, the way the overhead branches swept lower, sometimes scraping against the steel roof. He was grateful when the trees gave way to the moon–bleached fields and rocky hills.

It ought to be raining, he thought, taking a left at the first crossroads and rejoining the highway.

Gradually his head filled with memories, a layer of the senses, memories of good days spent behind the wheel of the Black Hawk, Sammy sticking his head out of the window and laughing infectiously as the wind rifled his hair, Francesca in the passenger seat clinging onto his waist for fear the boy might sprout wings and fly, fly away like the angel he was.

It really ought to be raining.

A whirlpool of dead leaves skittered down the center of the quiet track, twisting and skipping on the rutted gravel. A crumpled sheet of old news took flight before the car, cavorting with the leaves before being thrown into higher air, up over the roof and away. A red sun was poking through the fissures of cloud, revealing row after row of bleeding, blunted crop and painting gory slashes across the firmament of sky.

The sight of the sun's bleak progress behind the black silhouettes of gnarled boughs, shrunken limbs and defoliated fingers renewed Gabriel's feeling of anxiety; as if the Sun God's fiery eye swept the ground, looking for his hiding place amongst the mangled husks. There was no need to search his soul for reasons. He already knew the answer:

He was going home; the home he'd never had. No, that wasn't true. It was still his heart's home.

Montana.

The Reservation.

Gabriel looked at his dark eyes in the rearview, looking for clues as to how he felt.

The sound of gravel crunching under the roll of the Studebaker's tires grated on his frayed nerves. The road deserted, he took a left; taking the car out of the oppressive weight of trees, onto the steep decline of Split Crow Road. The long straight plunge into the Reservation. Gradually, as the car sped lower, the distant silhouettes changed into racks of caravans and trailers, clusters of campfires and clothes lines, tents and plyboard shanties. The blacked–out raven coup where Cry At The Moon cared for the sacred birds. Jeeps and pickups parked in the dirt, some carcasses of rust left out to feed the scavengers. Feathered dream catchers hung from trees ringing the valley, saving the dreams of his people from the White Man.

The magic doesn't work, he wanted to yell, to warn them, but they already knew. At least the gambling casinos hadn't made it this far, with their feral noses scenting out Federal land. He slowed the Black Hawk, taking it all in. This was his heritage. Here he was, last of the savages, as he mocked himself, driving a piece of the Americana that had destroyed an entire civilization with its creeping war of consumerism and plunder. Last rites and land rites, flintlocks and percussion pistols. His thoughts drifted back to the ageless women of Chinatown, locked stubbornly in their time warp, as he watched the hard–skinned hands of a woman in blue jeans wring out a cotton blouse and hang it out to dry. There was no need to ask her who had won the war for her native soil, she was wearing the brand name on her buttocks.

A bonfire was burning broken furniture and stuffed cushions. Kids played with sticks. A young girl sat on a caravan stoop, watching him openly as he drove slowly by. The ghetto blaster at her feet played some kind of funky saxophone he didn't recognize. She smiled, sorrow seeds planted in her sad eyes as her fingers drew her skirt slowly up her thigh. He shook his head, sighed.

Two rundown gasoline pumps sat in an island of sand, old fashioned, round–bodied pumps with heads like fishbowls and arrows for their smiles. A gecko had made its home in the belly of one, squatting in a bird's nest of twigs and dead leaves as if it had every right to be there. The lizard followed Gabriel with its eyes, long tongue licking out as he passed behind a trailer and out of sight.

Around the corner, an olive–legged girl in cutoff blue jeans was watching the world through the lens of a cheap–looking telescope; turned not to the stars but to the grit and the dust and the dirt of her own not–so–private Montana. When the glass eye found him, Gabriel touched his fingers to his lips and blew a soft breath over them as if they were sharing a kiss over some great distance. She ran a hand through her hair. Gabriel had to imagine her smiling at the other end of the telescope.

It really should be raining, he thought again, home now as he pulled up before a lightning–split tree adorned with colorful feathers and a spider's web of dream catchers. The dreaming tree, focus of the Reservation, the spiritual heart. He got out of the Studebaker, facing west, dust blurring his sight as he watched the marriage of desert and sky on the horizon. Closer to home a cluster of squalling seagulls bickered over freshly filled garbage bins. Gabriel concentrated on their primitive dance, fascinated by their naked savagery, wondering what had brought the scavengers this far inland.

He knelt, touching Mother Earth before smudging his fingers down the length of his nose and drawing parallel scars on both cheeks. Kissed his fingertips. Standing, Gabriel dusted his hands off on his Chinos.

His father was standing in the shadow of the doorway, the old man watching someone else's granddaughter play hopscotch in the dust in front of his trailer. His sleeveless J.C. Penney shirt was open on his huge barrel of a chest, the same spread–winged raven tattooed there, half–hidden by the shirt and the thick tangle of steel–gray hair. The little girl had dirt on her knees. He raised a clay pipe to his lips, drew in smoke and held his breath, held the smoke inside, as if he had no more need of air to breathe, then let it leak slowly out of his nose. Slowly, he tilted his head, as if listening to the sweet whisper of the wind. Gabriel had seen his father in the self same position, on the trailer stoop, listening, or so he said, to the Spirits of the Dead every day he was growing up.

When he was ready, the old man walked down the steps to welcome his son. "Star That Travels has found his way home," he said to the little girl, who giggled, and opened his arms.

Gabriel smiled and touched a finger to his lips, as if keeping a secret. "Don't tempt the Spirits, father. Don't invite a stranger into your home when he could be nothing less than your death come to reclaim you for First Father. There is blood on all of our hands, father. The sooner you learn that lesson, the better."

"Always had a smart mouth, didn't you, Star?" the old Black Foot said, remembering another time, another conversation, a parting instead of a greeting. Brushing aside the memory, he wrapped an arm around his son's shoulder. "Whatever your reason for coming," he gestured at the wide world with his clay pipe. "Welcome home, my son. Break bread with me. Tell me all of your stories."

THE men of the Black Foot sat stripped and cross–legged around the small fire. They had come to hear his story, mull it over and share their wisdom. It was the old way. A sharing of griefs under the Sky River where First Father and The Great Spirit could hear and heal the pains of the world.

Dusk was closing in over their heads.

Gabriel sat between Iron Bear and Sky Dancer. Iron Bear was the size of a great grizzly and just as unbending, whereas Sky Dancer was a wisp of a man, lithe and lightning fast, like the snake that strikes with poison fangs. They were the extremes of the Black Foot tribe, brute strength and sheer speed. For both men these deadly virtues were reflections of the personalities given to them by First Father. Not sim-ply names; they were their lives in words.

They sat in silence, drawing strength from each other's com-pany without the need for words, the fire danced like warm honey over exposed skin. Gabriel drew three circles in the dirt at his feet, one inside the other inside the other; the Trinity; the mark of the killer; the three that are one. It meant something. Something they were missing. He tried to catch hold of the thought but it was like one of those elusive Chinese finger puz-zles, the more he stared at it head–on the better it squirmed away from his understanding. He let his gaze settle on the flames, searching out a different kind of answer in their heat, but there was nothing, no secret lurking in the dancing fire.

Gabriel's father was the first to speak, his unlit clay pipe in his hand as he pointed across the flames at his son. "Star That Travels has found his way home with a story for us, my brothers." The old man's voice was deep, like the sound of hope being dragged across gravel. "A white skin's story of his new life away from his people." Gabriel closed his eyes waiting for the same ugly words, the same prejudices, to spill like bile from his father's lips. It isn't only the white men who nourish their hatreds, he thought bit-terly and bit down on the blackness rising up from his stomach. "He thinks that we should care. That we should share their hurts. After all the pain the white skins have inflicted on our fathers, on our brothers and sons with their lies and their guns. Their words, their lies, have oozed like thick black tar across the soul of the land. They are killers, that is their only truth." He let his words hang like smoke in the thick air. "That is the white skin's magic. Black tar lies that choke. And my son comes to us to ask for help on their behalf. I say we let the white skins drown in the tar pit they have made for themselves." The old man let it hang there for a second, stating a fact as if there was nothing left to say. No discussion to be had. "But it is my son's right to talk for himself. We may live in a world of the white skin's lies, but we may rise above them. Star That Travels, tell your story so that First Father may judge its worth."

A pale–skinned iguana scurried around the rim of the fire and scrambled up the bark of an ironwood tree, hanging upside down from one of its thorny branches. Somewhere in the distance, a train's siren sounded mournfully, its call haunting the sands.

Gabriel's fingers brushed over the head of his own raven tattoo. "I won't fight Wind Runner's wisdom. He is my father, and in much he is right. White man did us harm, and will do us more, we all know the lies he has told us, but as my father himself said: we must rise above them. This is my story, hear it and offer your wisdom without prejudice. For it is a story for all people, not just the white skins." He looked at the faces ringing the fire, for a sign of friendship in a single pair of eyes, but he was alone. He closed his eyes for a second, pressing his fingers against his temples, massaging them while he searched for the words.

Finally:

"A white man's death is stalking me, my brothers. His name is Lamenzo and I was with the men that killed him." Gabriel give his words a second to sink in. He looked across the flames at his father, Wind Runner. The old man's eyes were empty, no love, no hate, no emotion that he could see in their brown depths. "The truth is no story truly begins. As the story's teller I can only tell you where I stepped into it and hope you see the truth in my interpretation."

They nodded, the faces surrounding the fire, accepting the universal wisdom. No river has a source, we simply find ways to slip our bodies into its fast running water and taste its power for the shortest time.

It was no easier to tell the second time, to the doubting faces.

"It was in a church, beneath the eyes of their God. The boy had run for his life but still they took it. He was part of a street gang that worked for the wrong kind of people. Hired muscle."

"What does this have to do with us?" asked Red Fox Hunting, keen intelligence glittering within the flames that were his eyes.

"His last mortal act was the murder of a young girl," Gabriel replied, not really answering Red Fox Hunting's question. "He earned his death." Gabriel stopped talking, looked for a voice that was in some small way still his. A voice fit to talk about miracles and resurrections. "But he didn't die. Or rather he did die but an angel brought him back."

"How so?" Red Fox Hunting again, leaning forward intently.

"The wooden angel stepped down from its crucifix prison and breathed its own black life into his empty carcass. The breath of an angel brought the child killer back."

"Again I ask what bearing this has on the Black Foot, Star That Travels?"

Gabriel met the man's eyes across the fretful fire, found himself surprisingly steady, almost relaxed, resigned, as he said: "He recognized me. Read my soul. Left his fingerprints there, and his claws to dig and cut and hurt. This was three years ago, when the killing began. Three years when Lamenzo or whatever he became has walked in my dreams, tracking me, taunting me. I think...I think..." *I think, somehow, he killed my son...* "He has become the Angel of Death come to haunt me. I can feel him coming for me. Getting closer with each beat of my heart."

The gathered faces waited, giving Gabriel all the time he needed to focus the thoughts stacking up within his aching brain. He touched sensitive fingers to his temple again, feeling out the reassurance of blood, his pulse pumping, telling him he was still alive. He wanted to close his eyes but couldn't for fear of seeing Sam, seeing the dark angel of Lamenzo's shadow hovering over his dead son's soul, seeing those cadaverous fingers sinking like hooks into his innocent spirit.

"I do not fear for my own life," he said quietly, unable to look up, to meet their eyes this time. "I am no coward that runs from First Father's call. I fear the monstrosity that walks the streets of white man's finest creation. I fear the death of hope that trails in his wake. The end of all songs. All dreams. For he is death, not just to the white skins. This angel makes no discriminations for color. He dances to his own macabre tune. A plague bearer whose simple presence contaminates, kills. I have come home to seek the ancient wisdom of our people, to seek the magic that is my heritage, to find an answer, a way to fight this coldly stalking evil. I must. I cannot live through the nights he brings me, the sickness he stains my dreams with. I cannot deny my soul. I am Black Foot. I cannot stand and watch innocents die. I am Black Foot. It is my destiny to fight him. It is written in the Sky River."

"A disturbing story yours is, Star That Travels," Red Fox Hunting said softly, scratching fingers across his breastbone. The old shaman considered his next words carefully. "But this evil is no threat to our People. White skins and their gambling, their guns and their murdering ways are a threat to our lives. Are you hoping to move your people from the reservation, Star That Travels? To have them take up arms and follow your folly into the sky–touching houses of our enemy? To fight with them, side by side like blood brothers? Is that your wish? For that I cannot sanction. We are fighters no more. They have beaten the fight out of us, and that is the truth."

"I don't know what I am looking for, wise one. Only that I am a seeker, as I have always been a seeker. I come in search of answers to questions I do not yet know."

"Then, child of the ancient Sky River, you have not told us what we need to know to help form your questions. We have only heard words that offer no glory to the Black Foot. Tells us about this man Lamenzo and his angel."

"He was no one," Gabriel began again, trying to gather everything he knew about The Trinity Killer. Everything important and not. "We made a pact, those of us that witnessed his rebirth. It didn't happen. Not in our rational world. There was no room for this miracle. I think I had somehow forgotten about it because I didn't want to see it, didn't want it to be real, it was as if it had never happened.

"After my...after I lost my...my wife and son...after they died I stopped thinking about many things. I wanted to die. My soul yearned for it. And then the dreams came. He wore no face inside my head, so at first I didn't know him. But I knew his smell. It was on me. Marked me as one of his. But I didn't know him. I lost myself in my work, taking photographs, following people..."

He stopped talking and used his finger to scratch out the mark of The Trinity in the dirt.

"This is his mark. He has been taunting us with it. He murders a victim and scars them, carving this symbol into their flesh. It is the mark of the Trinity. Father, Son and Holy Ghost. Only there is no salvation in his cutting. It is a joke. I know it is. A cruel joke. Just like his arrival, coming down from their holy crucifix, mocking white man's faith. But I don't understand this joke...I took a photograph of a woman in a window...she had his mark on her cheek. Not when I saw her. Not when I took the photograph. The mark was in the actual print. A premonition of her death...I tried to warn her...to stop her...But she wouldn't listen...they found her body the next day."

"Her death is not on your hands, my son," Wind Runner said softly, reading the guilt in his son's eyes. "People live their lives and earn the right to die their own deaths. She chose not to listen. It was her choice. Her death as written in the Sky River."

"But I could have stopped it."

"No. You tried but her life was not yours to save."

"No."

"But you still want to save her don't you, Star That Travels, because you will be saving yourself. That is the story you have told us. If you could save her then you might live." Wind Runner nodded at Red Fox Hunting's words. "If she dies, then you die. And those around you die."

"But she is dead," Gabriel said with a voice he had no right to own. A voice that had sacrificed the one thing he had clung to for so long; clung to since Frankie and Sam's death. Hope.

FATHER Joe was rotting, the stiffness falling from his flesh like motes of dust. His head had lolled to one side so it looked as if he were staring at the mouse-trap beneath the table. Only the dead man couldn't stare because The Watcher had taped a garbage sack over his head, bound it up with an entire roll of masking tape.

The wet butt of a smoked out Cuban cigar sat in the ashtray next to the last of his 50–cent coins. The television was dancing to the colors and images of some pay–per–view porn flick. He couldn't concentrate on all that flesh with a dead man in the chair beside him. The Watcher coughed another tubercular cough and spat out a wad of yellowed phlegm.

"I'm sick," he said to Father Joe. "Cancer's inside me and it's eating me up, chewing its way out." He stared at the garbage bag head, hawked and spat again. "Like you give a fuck, right. Dead as a fucking doornail. Picked the wrong man to whine to, didn't I padre? Guess you think it's funny, don'tcha? Me worrying about cancer when there's a fuckin' Jesus Demon hunting me like I was some wild fuckin' rabbit. Yeah, I thought so. But the thing is, it's just a fuckin' race, right? See which death gets to me first, his or mine. I don't wanna die, padre. That's what bites. I really don't wanna die. Don't suppose you did either, did you?"

He grabbed a beer off the counter and turned back to the television. "This is fuckin' sick, don'tcha think, padre. Me watchin' a fuckflick with a dead guy? I never thought I'd end up like this, I sure as Hell bet Ma never saw this in the tea leaves. I was gonna be the Lone Ranger, the masked man who saved the fuckin' day. Some superhero, huh?" The Watcher popped the tab on the beer and chugged it down in one, foam and beer streaming out of both sides of his mouth as he opened his throat and swallowed. Down onto his shirt. Gasping, he wiped the back of his hand across his mouth and slammed the can down. "I needed that. Man, don't know about you, padre, but I've seen all the ass–fucking and ball sucking I can stomach. What say we kill the TV?"

He walked across the small room and pulled the plug on the box.

"Well, now what do we do for entertainment, padre? Not much of a talker are you? I guess we could listen to some music. What sort do you like? Jazz? Easy listening? Not that crap the kids are listening too? That's one hundred percent fucking attitude, zero percent music. Okay, let's see what we can find on the radio shall we?"

He'd found a no–brand transistor radio in the cupboard a couple of days ago. A cheap orange plastic thing. He fumbled with the dial until the sound of a wqiv talk–in jingle came through the tinny speaker, loud enough to fill the motel room with its mind–numbing melody. "I guess this'll have to do," The Watcher said, slumping down against the wall, by a small stack of empty cans.

The Shock–Jock's voice dopplered down, some kind of clever radio effect meant to make it sound scary. The effect was eerie and undeniably effective for all of its cheapness.

First song of the night, The Monster Mash. Let's kick the show off the old fashioned way. This is wqiv broadcasting into the heart of nyc. You're tuned in to the Nite Owls. Tonight we're going to be talking about ghoulies and ghosties and things that come bumping straight out of Wes Craven movies. For the next two and a half hours we're going to be taking an off–the–wall look at all things supernatural. Vampires, werewolves and zombies. The denizens of the night. The switchboards are open, the lights are flashing already. Had a true–life encounter with the paranormal? Feel like sharing it with us? Don't be shy, we're all friends here. Our number is 555-2684. This is going to be a good show, I can feel it. Okay, let's do the Monster Mash...

The Watcher reached for the phone, punched out the numbers and waited his turn. He smiled at Father Joe. The jingle cut in again and he heard, "Hello caller, you're through to the Nite Owls," through the phone seconds before he heard it on the radio.

"Hi, erm, look...I don't usually listen to your show. Don't much listen to the radio these days."

No problem. We can forgive you right? You're here now. Okay. So, first up, what's your name and what do you want to talk about?

"Right, I'd rather not say my name...you never know who could be listening, right?"

A laugh, then *Okay, play it your way. We need something to call you though, pal. Told you this was gonna be a good night.*

"You can call me The Watcher. It's what I do. I watch."

Whatever keeps the old cucumber hard, my friend. Talk away, we're listening.

"I want to talk about The Trinity Killer."

Think you got the wrong radio station, fella. This is the Monster Mash as in Bram Stoker and Anne Rice. Ain't no room for sickos on these here airwaves. Good clean family entertainment.

"Just shut the fuck up and listen to me. You might actually learn something."

sixty

DANIEL Mannelli listened to the taped conversation, then played it through again. The cold certainty in the man's voice was sickening. He could make out everything. The regular sigh of the man's breathing, his tongue catching on the wetness of his mouth. That wetness slowly drying out.

It was like having death whisper directly into his soul.

No. No, it was worse. This death was real. This death was tangible. Its chill was in the room with him, the sound of its voice like a shroud folding slowly over his soul.

He sat at his desk, back turned to the door, toying with a pencil, rolling it, pinching it between thumb and forefinger and tapping it against the mahogany–veneered armrests of his chair then he broke it with his fingers. He turned the chair around. Carefully, Mannelli replaced both halves of the pencil on the blotter.

Nik Lomas stood in the doorway, lurking like a Sicilian cleaner in his cheap suit and Gucci loafers. He swallowed a mouthful of quasi–espresso from a foam cup, shaking his head.

"The Police haven't got a fuckin' clue. He's got them on the run. New York's finest, my ass. They can't see shit because they don't want to. But me, I know. I've seen him with my own two eyes."

"–Whoa there, big fella. Let's just rewind that. You've seen the Trinity Killer? You know who he is? Is that what you're trying to tell me? You know who he is and instead of going to the law you come on a *radio* show?"

"Yes. I know who he is. I've seen him. I keep him in my sights. I watch him. It is what I do. I watch. I am The Watcher."

"Okay, okay, okay...Look, we've got to run some adverts. Will you stick around?"

"Play the adverts and I go. You won't hear the truth, New York. I know the truth. I want to spread the word. Kill the Jesus Demon they call The Trinity Killer. It is time for The Watcher to stop watching. Time for me to shed the skin of The Watcher, time for the beautiful Actor to emerge, to grow and live and feed off the daylight. Metamorphosis. We watch, we learn, we grow. I am growing. Can you hear me? I am growing. I am The Actor and

Death walks inside me."

In that last line the already gutteral voice twisted itself, hardening as it rasped out an animalistic snarl. Mannelli pushed himself to his feet and paced the floor. There were hollows under his eyes; he was pinched, face gaunt. His eyes themselves seemed glassy, blurring his window onto the world and the world's view of his soul. "You're a fucking psycho's what you are," he said, half to himself, half to a voice that had no way of hearing him.

"If you are out there, listening to this, Jesus Demon, I am coming for you. I am walking in your footsteps, cleaning up the mess you leave behind."

"Jesus Demon? You're losing me."

"Jesus Demon's what I call him. Saw him step down off a crucifix in St. Malachy's...saw it happen with my own fucking eyes, man. He ain't no Jesus. Jesus was an angel compared to this, this thing..."

"Right, Jesus was an angel...so, let me get this straight in my head...you've been cleaning up the Trinity Killer's mess since then?"

"That's what I said. Cleaning up his mess. I have been taking care of his leftovers. Walking in his shadow. Driving a stake through the heart of darkness. I've been cleaning up his mess. Sortin' them out so we don't get a plague of the motherfuckers is what I've been doing. I'm a regular fuckin' hero's what I am! Do you understand me?"

Lomas sank into a seat. He'd heard the tape through six times since the recording had come into his hands. The worst was yet to come and he knew it. They both did.

Mannelli spooled the tape forward.

"That's right...the last one, I found the last one in a hole. The Jesus Demon had got to him before I could stop him. It had his mark on its face. The mark of The Trinity. I had to cut its legs off with a hacksaw...do you know what it sounds like when you draw a hacksaw across bone? Do you?" There were sounds in the background, something heavy being dragged, falling. "It sounds like this, doesn't it Father Joe?" And there were more sounds now, the sounds of a saw cutting through flesh, meeting bone.

"Doesn't hurt does it, padre?" The voice was wheezing, out of breath. "I pulled its tongue out and cut out one of its eyes, too. Left it hanging on its cheek. Now that's one mother that isn't coming back, wouldn't you agree padre? I got another one of the bastards with my cheese wire. Pulled it so tight I could hear the windpipe ripping as the wire cut through its throat. Didn't bleed none, though. There should have been jets of blood when the arteries were sliced, and gurgled screams as its throat filled with blood. Not this one. Didn't make a sound, too far gone when I found it...

"Only bone stopped me taking its head clean off. Couldn't get the wire through...I had to do that with the hacksaw...now I know it ain't the same as a stake through the old ticker, but I ain't heard no complaining about the way I do things...you should be glad, all of you...I got 'em before they could get you, before they could come knocking at your door..."

"Where the hell did you get this, Nik? I hope to God it didn't go out on the air." Mannelli shook his head, lost, as he snapped off the small pocket recorder and sank back into his chair.

"A friend at WQIV. They pulled the plug on him. They record all of the shows as they go out. Got a time delay. Our friend here was replaced by an impromptu jingle and several words from happy sponsors. Was it right, what he said about the legs and stuff?"

"I only wish it wasn't, Nik. I only wish it wasn't."

AFTER Lomas left he played the tape through again, and again. His brow wrinkled as he tapped the end of the broken pencil against his teeth.

*Yesssssssssssssss...*he thought, the single word drawn out like a death sentence in his mind. *I know that voice from somewhere...I know I do...but where the hell do I know it from?*

Either someone had opened all of the windows in the squad room or something unnatural chilled him. Something about:

The voice...

"I'm a regular fucking hero's what I am."

The voice...

"A regular fucking psycho."

Where the hell do I know that voice from?

"SHE has the answers to your questions, Star That Travels."

"But she's dead," Gabriel said, not for the first time, finding no comfort in the obvious. He scratched anxiously at the raven tattooed into his breastbone. The sweat was peppering his forehead, clinging to his skin. Even the air, it seemed, was difficult to breathe. He felt lightheaded, weak from the fast. First Father demanded two days without food before communion could be granted. Gabriel held the flat of his hand against his collarbone, craned his neck, trying to sup the moisture from the air, trying to taste it on his parched lips as he waited for the hallucinations to begin.

"It is for you to seek the answers to your questions, to look beyond death. Seek her out on the Spirit Road. Seek out the dancing flame that is her spirit. Hear her call to you as you tread the fine line dividing existences. Your souls are twined, intertwined. One cannot but be drawn to the other." Red Fox Hunting offered Gabriel the gently smoking clay pipe in his hand. It smelled, not of tobacco, but of ginger and arrowroot. Scents to mask the true herbs tamped down in the pipe's bowl.

Gabriel drew deeply on the smoke, letting it leak out between tight lips. The taste was very different to the familiar bite of his licorice–skinned roll–ups. Sweeter. And it lingered even after he had passed the pipe on to Sky Dancer. Coils of smoke clinging to his tastebuds. Languid lovers offering him taste after taste. Sweet–faced succubi drawing him deeper into their sensual lair.

They had talked themselves around in circles, the words mirroring the maze that was The Trinity Killer's motif, first looking for answers then chasing down questions. All words led to one face. One body. One soul.

Charlotte Annuci.

Celine.

And as he kept trying to tell them, she was dead. He'd laid the first rose on her grave himself. Traced the lines of her name with his fingertip. He pictured her face, her ink–stain eyes and the strings of black pearls woven into her hair. Streetwise beauty laced with a hint of savagery. Thinking about her brought the smell of her perfume, a ghost scent drawn to the back of his throat as—

Something stretched taught across Celine's mouth and nose...her flattened lips paled...body bucked and thrashed about wildly under the weight but he rode her until there was nothing left...her face cold and dead against his groin, where the whole erotic dance had started...colors danced...glittered like the blade of a knife...cutting, cutting, cutting...carving the shape of a tree into her belly, opening her up lips to lips...unravelling her, laying the gray coils of intestine out like so many umbilical cords looping back to the tree of life...carving the image of a pregnant man on her left cheek, smeared the blood into a halo...

—he began losing sense of himself, felt himself moving, spinning without moving as the colors flashed across his clouding eyes. Tasted fear as the bizarre dance gripped his soul. A rainbow dance of colors.

"Feel the dirt beneath you, cling to it. It's your way home." Was it a voice that spoke to him? "Seek out her soul, she is the answer to your questions...seek out her flame. Listen, hear its call...hear its lament."

Gabriel's mind danced with the impossibility of rainbows, butterflies or things like butterflies, fragments of dizzying color that beat their insectlike wings and blinded him, lifted him, carried him into the music, the primordial drumbeat of The First Song, the eerie chanting of the dead, the joyous whisper of the yet–to–live, left him floating on a current of color.

He reached out with his hands, but had no hands, not in this place. Not when his sight tried to focus on the bulk of his body. He was light, a flame of pure silver light that danced to the music of life. He felt the presence of other soul–flames drawing close to his light; Sky Dancer's shimmering azure, Red Fox Hunting's aura a brittle egg of cobalt, the shape of the old shaman's body just visible within it. Gabriel tried to focus on the few memories he had of the sad–faced Charlotte, the physical and the ephemeral. The faintest trace of rose–scented shampoo came to him as he drew her face inside his mind's eye, slowly painting in the ink stains of her eyes.

His mind soared, his soul–flame chasing towards those dark pools. His voice, when he called to her, was swallowed, drowned by the beautiful shimmering song that was eternity. As the notes chimed within his mind, each one like the birth of bright stars, the sparks of new soul–flames burned into life.

Beneath him, somehow, he felt the cold dirt on his skin, wanted to let go, to fly, fly in those eyes.

"Feel the dirt beneath you," the no–voice hissed. "Cling to it or we are all lost." And that held him, anchored him.

There were so many soul–flames, so many hues and shades, subtle and bright, blinding and muted.

Charlotte, he called out with his heart. Celine. Charlotte? And inside a fading flame he saw her

—on her knees...a hand raised to her lips as if his semen has somehow burned her...laughter...harsh...braying laughter...as a hand snatches up a fistful of her hair...jerks her backwards...onto her back...kicks her legs out from under her...slaps her across the face...punches her in the throat...hard...can't breathe...gasping for air that isn't there...

—face twisting into a scream, an agony of blood ruining her beautiful eyes.

He wished himself towards her, spirit drawn like a moth to her dying flame. The dizzy euphoria Gabriel had tasted only seconds before was gone now, the colors fading, first to die the blue of the summer sky, the gold of the sun, a forest of greens, as one after another the illusion of soul–flames brutally burned out.

Somewhere around him, near, inside him, Red Fox Hunting's scream tore through the blackness.

Gabriel was alone in the darkness.

He reached out with his senses for the coldness of the dirt beneath his buttocks but it was gone.

We're the same, you and me...

We're the same...

He felt himself floating on the sea of someone else's agony, through the river of their hurts, the fast rushing waters of their life threatening to engulf him; Barbis's cheap cologne, Father Joe smiling as he lit another candle, mom in tears, dad drunk himself into a coma, his hands pressing down, pressing down, Rosie Bossman's dead eyes looking up through the suffocating pillow. The surge of memories kept coming; the lovers in his bed, the broken glass of the crack pipe, the crumpled notes and fake smiles. A silver web of souls, a tapestry of faces, carved in masks of death. Faces that belonged to them all, dead and alive and dying. He was losing himself. Had to struggle to break free. To twist and fight and throw off the memories before they were all he had left. And still they swallowed him; the car cruising the street, the unfortunate with her braids of pearls, her hands on his buckle, lips on his cock, taking him in.

And he knew her, he knew her, he knew her…

Charlotte, his spirit cried out, but she was gone, snatched from him. He was left staring at himself, at his reflection in the empty soul–flame, and he was Lamenzo but he wasn't, not completely. He was…he was…a name…a face…black bird…foot…Gabriel. He was Gabriel. He clung to that shred of identity knowing somehow it was all there was of him left in this world. In any world.

Lamenzo's face shimmered, losing definition, sharp edges.

"Listen to the song," Red Fox Hunting's no voice whispered to him from somewhere in the black. Then he felt the touch of ice and fire, the burning pain of spirit–death as Lamenzo reached beyond the edges of his soul–flame. "Quickly," The voice urged. "Open your mind to the notes. Feel them."

He tried, but Lamenzo's fingers kept dragging him back to the pain. Fingers suddenly clawlike, jags of red glass–bone. The sensations built quickly. The first faint flowering of pain nothing against the growth of agony that marked Lamenzo's fingers closing around his pumping heart, squeezing the straining valves.

"Illusion," the voice hissed. "Fight it. Fight the—"

And yet the searing bursts of pain were intense. The blood inside the straining walls of his forcibly–stilled heart surged up against the dam–like valves, the wash of the red tide advancing within him, needing to give way, to burst…

"—ILLUSION!" the sudden explosion of sound shattered the claws, fragments of glass and bone spinning off into the black. Lamenzo reached out again, the jags of bone–glass reforming as they raked across the cusp of Gabriel's soul–flame.

He spun away, the dirt suddenly very cold beneath his buttocks. "How do I get back?" he yelled frantically, tasting his fear in the dead air all around him. "How the hell do I get back?"

"Open your mind to me, reach out, feel the dirt of the earth, taste the air, the smoke, see your body, your face…"

Lamenzo's soul–flame was burning up, the colors shifting crazily, burning up through the spectrum to an all consuming red.

Gabriel tried to focus his thoughts on the single shred of identity he'd somehow managed to cling to, tried to pull himself back into his name, to relearn himself, his face, his body. Felt himself drawn. Falling.

But still the thing that was Carlos Lamenzo came for him, the borrowed flesh falling away from its blazing form, peeling back on its skin of fire, its flesh of red hate–flame. Sparks burned angrily, the conflagration fanned by hate, lust, need, desire, pain, spanning across the black, burning for him. Burning for Gabriel.

I can taste your soul, Indian. I can taste it on my tongue. You're mine. You always have been...

But he was gone, the rush of ecstasy, exhilaration, life hurling him back towards the empty shell that was his body.

I'm dying, Gabriel thought, locked in the memory of gunshots; bullets taking him in a rush of agony, upper thigh, groin, abdomen, cheek, spleen, lungs, heart, and arm. The dance of death they forced his dying–dead–body into even as he tried to stand. The bark of more shots, the icy cold of St. Malachy's. The punches came again, in the chest, temple, leg. The touch of something cold, glass, on his hand...

He touched tentatively at his face, feeling for the pits of decay beneath the desiccating skin, but felt soft flesh. Felt the scar on his left cheek. Gabriel's scar.

Gabriel's scar. Not his. He wasn't Gabriel. He was...he was...but his name, the very core of his identity danced seductively on the edge of reason, tantalizingly close but out of reach.

He swallowed down the bile, the fear, and opened his eyes.

He wasn't in the church, wasn't bleeding, wasn't dying. He was sitting, cross–legged and stripped naked, beside Red Fox Hunting and Sky Dancer, baking in the heat of the sweat. Beads of perspiration peppered his skin. Gabriel was aware, vaguely, that the memory of St. Malachy's wasn't his. He knew the scene, had pulled one of the triggers. But every time he'd lived in that memory he'd been on the outside of the ring, looking in, doing the killing.

But in this memory, in this insistent memory, he was on the inside of the ring, feeling the death offered by the bullets, tasting Lamenzo's confusion and fear even as the angel claimed his soul.

"Welcome home, Star That Travels." The voice was Sky Dancer's. Gabriel had to fight the urge to say that wasn't his name; to say that his name was Carlos Lamenzo. But it wasn't. His name was...the scar on his left cheek...Gabriel's scar...his name was Rush...Gabriel Rush. He pressed his fists into his temples, as if trying to drive Lamenzo's thoughts, memories, out of his head. Because bullets weren't the only thoughts, the only memories he shared with The Trinity Killer,

"Lamenzo's florists, Ma'am. Got a bouquet for you." he said, tasting the goodness of the lie. The rightness...waited...opened the door...he smiled at his reflection in the glass...yes, yes...rounding the first flight of stairs...talking to the hunger inside him...the

door...5A...

there were others. Others much closer to home. The phone that rang unanswered. He could see her face in the collage of victims and didn't know whose memory he was trawling, but he didn't need to, he could taste Lamenzo's hunger on his tongue. The need that gnawed at his guts, drove him on.

"Ash," he said sickly, struggling to stand with the need—the same need—suddenly, desperately driving up through him. "Ashley."

"What is it?"

"He's got her...oh God...he's got Ashley."

"How do you know?"

Gabriel clutched at his scalp suddenly, tearing at it, clawing, trying to open it up. "Because he's in here..." he yelled then, the heels of his hands jamming into his temples. Twisting. "He's in my head."

DULL light slithered over the page, throwing its shadows over the words of the coroner's report. Words he knew too well. Descriptions of savagery that he didn't need photographs to visualize.

Daniel Mannelli thumbed over the page, swallowing a mouthful of lukewarm coffee, tasting it leak down his throat like treacle. The face of Caroline Öberg smiled up at him in one shot. Her mutilated corpse bled for him in the black–and–white beside it. He could hear the squad room busy with subdued life.

He shifted his glance towards the window, his thoughts drifting through the plate glass and out onto the street, seeking out The Trinity Killer and his elegiac cortege.

He stood, paced, sat again.

And not for the first time he found his thoughts chasing around the rabbit–warren of murky streets and murkier crimes that were described so accurately by The Watcher.

Questions he had, but no answers to go with them. Where did he learn so much about the killings he described, the mutilations? A handful of detectives had been trusted with truth about the garrotings and dismemberments, no words for the Press, no hints to the blackly macabre side of The Trinity's nature. Murders and murderers there were aplenty, the number of active serial killers in the States alone had peaked at over eighty in the last month, but this kind of killing, this brutal vivisectionist nightmare, this was a taboo limited to single figures. The damaged killers whose psychoses and neuroses drove them into the arms of depravation.

But slowly things had begun adding up; after Brendon Ellery's call to Delgado, his copycat theory, The Watcher's cleaning up made a sick kind of sense. Not a copycat killer. A street cleaner who lacked the subtle artistry of the man he followed. A man killing the dead because his own demons insisted they would rise again.

Mannelli reached around for the tape recorder, suddenly needing to hear the voice again, knowing it and knowing he knew it.

"Doesn't hurt, does it, padre?" Bill Stern wheezed at him.

sixty five

THE angel–fed corpse of Carlos Lamenzo pulled his teeth away from the motorway of capillaries that was the dead policeman's neck and inspected his handiwork.

The need was still upon him, no matter the blood staining his lips, the carrion settling in his stomach; there was no slaking it, no end to the craving. He wanted more. Needed more. Needed to know that they were empty, like him, the dead men he was hunting. The last witnesses to his miracle. This one lying in his hands left two more for his cull, the little Indian and the fat man.

He could taste their fear even this far away from them, but when he closed his eyes, when he thought about the Indian and his gun, when he smelled the journey of his bullet, the images were all wrong, confused. Death was flowing backwards, away from him and into the corpse of Lamenzo.

But he was Lamenzo, at least a part of him had fed on all that was left of the child killer. He was an angel...he was Gabriel...no, no...he was...he was...the Angel of Red...the Angel of Pain.

Suddenly, the image of a woman flowered, the face of the woman he loved...no, the face of the woman the little Indian loved...his dead smell was all over her.

He pushed himself up, fighting the need to feed, the need to taste more of the dead man sprawled at his feet.

It was her his soul hungered for. Her soul that would quell the need. Take the hunger away.

Sweet Ashley.

"Oh Jesus Christ, Jesus Christ, Jesus Christ."

Mannelli slammed the open palm of his hand into the plaster wall. The shockwaves were still chasing down the bones seconds later as he opened the squadroom door. Standing there, Stern's voice taunting his back, he yelled for Delgado: "Jack, get in here now and tell me this isn't who I think it fucking is!"

Delgado looked up from his two-finger typing, pinched at his nose, pulling on the wiry hair growing out of his nostrils, and pushed his chair back. He was a big man, suited to life in a chair. He walked slowly, trying to look over Mannelli's shoulder into the empty office, looking for the person he was supposed to be identifying.

He could hear Bill Stern's voice. That familiar, gruff New Yorker's burr. Odd, he thought, glancing across at the clutter of foam cups littering the detective's otherwise empty desk. He hadn't noticed Stern come in. Sick, he was supposed to be. Stomach flu. Hadn't been around since the autopsy on Father Joseph D'Angelo.

"What is it, Chief?" he asked, popping his shoulder–joint as he stretched, working the blood through the old bones. Mannelli, he saw, was clenching his right hand in his left, as if nursing it.

"Just listen," Mannelli said, still blocking the doorway. "Tell me what you hear. Everyone else," he yelled again, "shut the fuck up for twenty seconds. I want silence."

But there wasn't silence, because in it, where it should have been, Bill Stern said: "I'm a regular fucking hero…that's what I am…"

"I thought you were too sick to be coming in, Billy–boy?" Delgado said, trying to look past Manneli at the fat policeman who wasn't there.

"Fuck," Mannelli spat. "Fuck fuck fuck fuck." He spun on his heel and slammed the office door only to emerge with a tape recorder in his hand, the tape spooling backwards so he could play Bill Stern's radio appearance to the whole squad room, looking for one person to say no, it wasn't Stern at all. That he was wrong, that they all were. He pressed play:

"…Jesus Demon they call The Trinity Killer. It is time for The Watcher to stop watching. Time for me to shed the skin of The

Watcher, time for the beautiful Actor to emerge, to grow and live and feed off the daylight. Metamorphosis. We watch, we learn, we grow. I am growing. Can you hear me? I am growing. I am The Actor and Death walks inside me..."

Movement stopped. A torpor of disbelief slowly folded itself around the people in the room as they listened to their friend describe the killings, the mutilations, and his twisted role in them.

"I want this sick fuck found, do you hear me? I want him found and I want him finished."

Behind him, in the office, his telephone rang.

HE waited, cold on the street corner, for someone to open the door to her building, for someone to open the door and let him in, let him in so the dance could begin.

"Can I help?" he asked a pale–skinned woman, as she juggled shopping bags and struggled with the door.

"Thanks," she said, letting him take the door.

Smiling, he let himself in behind her.

This close, the need twisted around his stomach like a hungry fist, pulled at his guts like sickness. He climbed the stairs in the grip of it, tasting her smell on the air, knowing it was her the need cried out for, knowing that she could at least bring an end to his hunger.

5A.

He knocked once and waited, running a hand across his cheek, feeling out the deep wounds where his flesh was failing, where the need was killing this body again. Behind the door, he heard the purposeful bustle of footsteps and out–of–tune humming as the guard chain was slipped into place.

The door cracked open.

"Yes?" Ashley, his Ashley…no…no…the little Indian's Ashley… asked through the four–inch crack.

"Miss Powell?" he asked, a confident, antiseptic smile slipping easily over his crumbling features.

"Yes, can I help you?"

"I sincerely hope so, Miss Powell, almost as much as I hope to help you." His voice dripped with too–sweet honey. "My name is Lamenzo, Carlos Lamenzo." He held out a hand to be shaken.

"What can I do for you, Mr. Lamenzo?" she asked, ignoring his outstretched hand.

"I'm a salesman, Miss Powell, but," he purred, "before you slam the door I think you ought to hear what it is I am selling, don't you?" She didn't move. "Heaven," he crooned. "That's my product. I'm selling tickets to heaven. Now, you can't refuse an offer like that, can you?"

"Sounds…delightful," she replied. "Perhaps some other life."

"Your loss," he said as she closed the door on him.

SHE closed the door on the salesman of God and moved back into the kitchen to fill the glass coffee pot with columbian roast. On the windowsill the radio played away to itself, Dave Matthews' voice lost behind the bubble of water boiling on the stove. Turning the volume up, she dismissed her visitor as just another one of New York's colorful cranks. Harmless but crazy.

A bunch of dried flowers had collapsed on the draining board, stalks and stems waiting for the knife to trim them for the vase. "Carlos Lamenzo," she said quietly, pulling at a string that had twisted itself around one of the thorny stems. The dried stalk snapped in her clumsy fingers.

"The flowers...the flowers never came."

Behind her, in the passage, she heard Lamenzo hurl himself at the door, heard the dry cracking of it beginning to splinter inwards, the sudden scream of the guardchain's mounting being ripped from its wooden bed. Another kick and the splinters were splintering.

She scanned the kitchen frantically for some kind of makeshift weapon. The long bench was littered with utensils and half–prepared salad. Her eyes trembled across a fan of knives, lingering on a thin–bladed carver, its arrogant silver sheen already bloodied with the juices of a beet.

She grabbed at the knife, her heart hammering against her breastbone, and sent it skittering off the benchtop onto the linoleum floor. "Oh Jesus, oh Jesus..." Quickly, she stooped to recover it, her hand closing around its comforting metal strength. It felt good in her hand. Reassuringly heavy. *Heavy enough to gut a salesman of God,* she told herself.

GABRIEL pressed the receiver up against his ear, jammed a finger in the other, trying to shut out the rabble of voices swarming every which way. "Dan?" he half–shouted as the public address system, in the form of a soft, sensuous voice, announced the discovery of a lost child. A family clad in gaudy palm tree–print shirts squawked Pidgin English between mouthfuls of cheeseburger. They stopped for a portrait beside the onyx fountain. Gabriel tried to tune them out.

The AT&T phone booth was sandwiched between a row of glassy–eyed Photo–Me booths and a newspaper rack that seemed to have simply spilled its copies of *The Herald Tribune* and *The Guardian International* out onto the airport's marbled floor. Monitors hanging from the ceiling displayed the departures and arrivals. His flight back to New York was boarding.

"Mannelli," he sounded down, on the point of breaking.

"Dan? It's Gabriel," he said quickly, his words trying to race the feeling of inevitability that was slowly stifling him. He'd walked out on Ashley, thrown himself into this fool's quest, left her to whatever the thing was that shared his head.

"We got him, Gabe." Mannelli said, voice flat, dead. Those three words set his heart soaring. Unconsciously, he searched through the few memories he'd held on to that belonged to The Trinity Killer, but no, there was no recollection of capture in there. No arrest. It must have happened after their separation. "You've brought him in?"

"It was Stern, Gabe. Bill fuckin' Stern. That man was like, shit he was like my father only he was better, you know."

Stern? No...that was wrong. From soaring his heart swooped, swollen and threatening to burst in a wash of blood–red pain, so cruel for its suddenness. "Dan, listen to me. It's Ashley. He's going after her. Don't ask how I know. I've been trying to call her but I can't get through. She's not picking up. You've got to get her out of that place, Dan." He closed his eyes but couldn't keep them closed because of what he saw

in her hand, the edge of metal...a knife...on her knees...

"He's there...Jesus, I know he's there and I can't get to her. I'm ten fucking hours away. You've got to help me."

LOOKING up, she saw a pair of stained neubuck boots standing in the kitchen doorway. Breathing slowly, fighting to stay calm, Ashley moved her eyes upwards, over a pair of ripped denims and to an off–white linen shirt to then to his face.

Lamenzo held out his right hand. "We can do this the easy way," he said, smacking his dry lips together and making a show of holding out his left hand. "Or we can do it the hard way. Up to you. Easy? Hard?"

Her hand closed tighter around the hilt of the knife, knuckles blanching white with the strength of her grip, and slowly, oh so slowly, she brought it up to her side.

"My, my," Lamenzo chuckled. "You actually want to do it the hard way? Damned shame, fine looking piece of meat like yourself, getting all cut up." He stepped forward, shaking his head sadly, a direct contrast to the brittle–looking grin that cracked his face from ear to flaking ear.

A jumble of a million idiot things cluttering her mind, Ashley tensed, the muscles around her calves bunching painfully, readying themselves for a sudden cat–like lunge with the knife.

"You know I didn't want to hurt you." Lamenzo's lie was smooth, the salesman's mask still in place. Almost believable.

"Much," Ashley hissed, springing forward and thrusting the blade's point up, aiming for the bulge in his jeans. Lamenzo shrieked, one arm snaking out to parry the lunge, the other darting down and grabbing at a tangle of her hair. Both missed.

The knife flew out of her sweating palm, skittering and spinning across the floor before coming to rest beyond the arched entrance into the passage. "Oh, God." It was a whimper, indistinguishable from the ragged gasp of breath that birthed it. Shuffling desperately backwards, her knees scraping and sticking to the warm linoleum, her eyes never leaving his face, Ashley reached out blindly for another weapon; anything. Her back pressed up against the cold Formica of the drainer as it cut off her retreat. Without thinking, she pushed against it, used its unrelenting solidity to move painfully to her feet.

He stepped slowly closer, rictus grin betraying his hunger, his need.

On the drainer, Ashley's trembling hand closed around the blue glass vase; the empty vase waiting for the dried flowers.

"Oh, sweet Ashley. I said I didn't want to hurt you...but look what you've made me go and do. You've made me kill you." Lamenzo's eyes seemed to glitter, sparkle, filled with tears of fresh–blown glass. "I really didn't want to kill you, I really didn't... but now I'm gonna rip your fuckin' heart out, bitch!"

She didn't wait for him to come for her, she hurled the vase. It turned end over end, and smashed into his face, leaving the swell of a shattered nose as it broke.

Shrieking, Lamenzo's hands clasped over the bridge of his nose as he staggered back into the refrigerator door.

"Strike three, motherfucker!" Ashley yelled, darting beneath his ineffectual swipe, "And you're out!" The knife had spun away under the arch of the telephone stand, just far enough under that she had to stretch to reach it. Behind her Lamenzo wailed again. Her heart thudding like a derailing locomotive, Ashley groped for the knife, her fingers catching empty air.

Then she had it.

The Trinity Killer stood in the kitchen archway, glass eyes glazed and unfocussed; still obviously disorientated from the shock of the blow. Taking hold of the carver with both hands, Ashley lunged at him again.

Too slow, he tried to grab a fistful of her hair, less adroitly than before but with more success. Laughing, Lamenzo yanked her head backwards, the motion jerking her body around so Ashley was forced to look up at him in a parody of supplication. Gazing into her frightened eyes, for this moment her God, her universe, her life in his hands, Lamenzo felt the knife's wicked edge slice along his bare forearm, felt it peel back the dry layers of dead flesh and then it was burying itself fist deep between his legs, its tip severing the thickness of his femoral artery, twisting, gutting him. A sudden, shocking fire burned hatefully out from the gaping wound blazing up into his heart in a second.

He staggered, legs giving way; not used to the pain, not used to the fragility of his borrowed human skin; fingers clasping and unclasping reflexively, losing their tangled grip on Ashley's hair. Lamenzo's body lurched away from the angel's control, fell clumsily backwards into the archway as his hands closed around the carver's wooden hilt.

"Bitch," he wailed. "You dumb fuckin' bitch." And toppled forward on to his knees, just inches from her face.

For eternity he hung there, suspended, his slate–gray eyes bitter winter mist as they bore into her soul, tasted her flame, caught it, fed themselves. To Ashley, on the outside looking in, there were clouds suddenly in that winter sky, clouds that dulled the fire of the dead man's life, claiming him once again for their own, and he fell the rest of the way to the floor, driving the knife deeper into his bloody genitals.

The dead man released a last baleful lament before silence claimed him. The sound, as hateful as it was, seemed almost to be echoed inside her own head.

Sobbing, Ashley crawled crab–like away from Lamenzo's body, pushing herself into a corner, shoulder–blades pressed hard against the Formica drainer, back where it began and unable to take her eyes from the growing puddle of red leaking onto the linoleum tiles and the bloody bubble that had been made by her attacker's dying breath.

Above her, the coffee pot began to boil itself dry.

BILL Stern, The Watcher, sat outside, in his car, doing what he did: watching.

He sucked on the thick end of a cuban cigar, breathing out fire. No smoke without fire, he told himself wryly as he looked up at the rows of blind windows. He had been forced to leave Father Joe back at the Paradise Motel, bound up in a few garbage sacks and smelling bad. Give the cleaner a surprise.

Gaze resting on the fifth floor window again, it seemed fitting that this was what he had spent most of his life doing; watching. Waiting.

The Jesus Demon was up there, he knew, and this time the watching was done, this was the hour of The Actor.

Ducking down against the Coupe's steering wheel, he reached under the driver's seat, dirt stained fingers clawing out and hooking around the smooth surface of a half–empty bourbon bottle. Pulling it up, Stern twisted off the cap and swallowed a sharp, tangy mouthful. The liquor was lukewarm going down but its innate fire spread a soothing warmth through his stomach. Twisting the cap back on, he kicked the bottle back under the seat and looked back up at the window again, still putting off the moment.

Still no sign, no outward giveaway that the Jesus Demon was working its evil magic inside the apartment block.

He leaned across to the passenger seat, lifting one of the sharpened stakes out of the open toolbag and rolling it between his hands. The bag, his work bag, contained the few essentials he'd needed to get this far: the saws; the stakes; a claw hammer; Geronimo, his six–inch hunting knife with serrated edge; a garrote; and an album of collated cuttings from newspapers and police files dating back over three long years.

DANIEL Mannelli slammed the handset down into its cradle, grabbed his jacket from the back of the chair and ran through the detective squad room ignoring the stares that greeted him. For all the joking, he knew better than to question Gabriel's feelings.

"Delgado, Lambert, Kolchak," he shouted, naming the first faces he saw. "Grab your coats. We've got him. The Reisinger Building on Prospect."

He didn't wait to see if they were following. Took the stairs three risers at a time, hand sliding down the rail. The sound of his footsteps echoed hollowly in the concrete trap of the stairwell. Coming into the Muster Room at a run Mannelli slammed into an unhappy prostitute waiting to be led away. Rouged lips twisted in an ugly smear as she kissed her middle finger in his face.

"Where's the fire, Mannelli?" The desk sergeant called from his lofty perch. Of late happiness wasn't a condition Mannelli had been particularly familiar with, but for all that familiarity, the twist of anguish he felt as he spoke was suprisingly acute:

"Put out a call for backup, we've got him. The Reisinger Building on Prospect." The look on his face was enough to have the desk sergeant picking up his radio mike and sending out the call without asking who.

His Three Musketeers, Delagado, Ross Lambert and Dale Kolchak ran straight through the Muster Room, Lambert still shrugging into his leather jacket as he ran. Mannelli followed them out through the glass double doors and into the street. The first snowflakes were falling, wrapping the air in white. A fairy tale Christmas in New York.

The worn leather soles of Mannelli's shoes slipped on the damp stone.

SHE listened for familiar sounds within the nightmare:

The radio, the bubble of the coffee pot, the hum of the refrigerator, sounds that could wrap her in a cocoon of normality, sounds that could breathe life back into the real world.

Sounds that denied the salesman of God lying dead on her floor.

She felt sickness climbing in her throat, felt the bitter tang of it clawing to be free. Ashley closed her eyes but instead of blackness and escape there was a death called Lamenzo dancing where there should have been darkness and safety. She opened her eyes again, knowing what was waiting for her when she did, but still sickened by the spreading circle of blood.

She began to move, needed to.

Tremors chased along the muscles of her arms as Ashley crawled oh so slowly past the body of her would–be killer, the warmth of his blood making gloves for her hands as they walked through his death. And in that elastic moment she found herself vomiting, putting her hands up to her face and screaming as the blood sank in. She couldn't move for the longest time and even when she could it was a slow, torturous struggle that took her face to within inches of his. She the Moon and him the Earth, her orbit brought their lips into a lover's proximity, hovered as if addicted to the gravity his body imposed on hers.

Then she was in the passageway, past Lamenzo's body, and the spell was broken. She felt a wetness between her legs, spreading through her sweatpants, a dark wet stain around the joint of her legs and down her thighs. "Oh, fuck..."

The phone was on a stand just inside the hall and mercifully out of sight of Lamenzo's corpse. Pressing her back against the wall, Ashley lifted the telephone into her lap. She didn't know who to call, she knew Gabe had friends on the force, she could see a line–up of faces, but no names.

She sniffed. She had started to cry without realizing it.

Outside she heard the sound of a car door slamming and young people laughing as they walked up the street towards the river.

"Pull yourself together, girl. You're tough. You're a survivor." But she didn't feel tough and she didn't feel like a survivor. She felt like the victim of a hit–and–run. She felt like roadkill.

Shivering, she plucked at the sweatpants where they clung to her thigh. The hallway, her hallway inside her home, suddenly felt cold and unfriendly.

She pressed out the numbers 911. The first bleat had scarcely sounded when a calm voice said: "Emergency Services. Which service do you require?"

"Help me," she said, barely a whisper. Drawing her knees up to her chest she slipped into a kind of comfortable cradle and began rocking slightly, the phone still held to her mouth but her mouth unable to form the words she so desperately wanted to say as the shock settled in and began suffocating her.

"Are you still there, miss?"

She tried to say yes. Nodded.

"Is there someone in the apartment with you?"

Again she tried to say yes; something came out but it wasn't a word.

"Listen to me. Stay calm, if you can get out of the building, get out. Do not put yourself in danger. Understand."

"His...his body...body's in the kitchen." she said finding the truth inside her somehow, giving voice to it. "I think he's dead...I think...I think I killed him."

From downstairs she heard the sound of the main door swinging closed and the security lock latching into place, followed by the slow, measured sound of footsteps coming up the stairs.

"Okay, sit tight. Don't touch a thing. Don't move a thing until we get an officer on the scene. Can you confirm One Eleven Prospect Parkway and I will dispatch paramedics and officer back-up."

"Yes."

"And your name?"

"Oh God, I think I killed him."

"Your name please, miss?"

"Ashley. Ashley Powell."

"Okay, Miss Powell, there are officers on their way. Don't let anyone into or out of the building before they arrive."

"All right," she said.

She put the phone down and stood, looking around as if she

were in some stranger's house, as if everything around her belonged to someone else, some other woman who lived the kind of life that had room for pools of blood and dead bodies in the kitchen.

"Gabe," she said, needing to talk to him, to hear his voice say everything was going to be all right.Starting to shake again, she looked at the small black bottle of Sandman sandwiched between the three bottles of malt and rye on the bookcase. She thought about going back into the kitchen for a glass but there was his body on the floor and all that blood. So much blood. No, she decided, no glass.

She unscrewed the cap and raised the bottle to her lips.

As she swallowed the short hairs on the nape of her neck bristled beneath the electricity of instinct's caress. She felt him in her throat even as she looked around frantically for the knife she'd left in the kitchen, left imbedded in him.

Behind her, a wet, shuffling sound like dragging feet, and then something else, another sound. Raw. Wet. Meat being torn. Brittle cracks. Bones being pulled back on themselves and broken.

"Just answer me this one question, bitch. Do you want to live?"

Turning her head, too late to run, she saw too much. The Angel within Lamenzo's body was shedding its borrowed skin, peeling back the dead flesh. Opening its secret anatomy with claws, touching the corruption of the child killer's corpse, parting the clotted muscle and slowly bleeding death onto the carpet as, layer by layer the angel peeled away a miracle. A cage of white bone beneath the flesh, and then like some groteseque butterfly the angel began the screaming agony of its rebirth, coming out from the skin, breaking the white cage bone by bone, taking Lamenzo off just as easily he would a suit of light. It stepped out of the corpse, leaving the carapace of skin and bone in a bloody wet puddle around its ankles. A sheen of blood clung with lover's intimacy to the angel's true form, blood that ran a wash of red through its hating eyes.

Ashley backed up a step, already dead without the motors of her heart and lungs realizing the redundancy of beating.

The angel stepped forward a step, reaching out, a curious, almost childlike gesture as if it needed help taking its first few faltering steps. It was drawing agonized gasps, as if being born again had truly hurt it. Then it was moving with more certainty; a purpose. Claws that should have been fingers pushed into her, gripped her, pulled her close so that the sting of the angel's overly sweet breath brought tears to her eyes.

"Do you want to live?"

She thought of Gabriel then, in that fraction of a second as a sharp stabbing pain flowered in her kidneys. The Angel's claws opened her skin, parted the striated layers of muscle and tendon in search of the ultimate prize; her heart. And then her legs were folding, balance betrayed by the intimacy of death.

"Do you want to live?" It asked again, tasting her delicious fear. Tasting the bitter tang of hope in her heart, the flutterings of love for the Indian. He waited out her screams, waiting for the answer he knew memories and love would bring to his ears. Of course she wanted to live.

Her screams faded as her face kissed the softness of the carpet. She pushed her hands beneath her, struggled to rise but weakness, cool like the elixir of nevermore, flowed through her veins and she slumped back to the floor...the carpet smelled stale of burned–out cigarettes and blood.

"Yes," she said, or tried to say as the life leaked out of her, *I want to live. I want to live...sorry, Gabriel, I'm so sorry...I'm so sorry...*

HALFWAY up the second flight of stairs he heard the woman's screams and knew he was too late.

The faint blush of a breeze tasting him felt weary with the knowledge of death, its condition contagious.

Bill Stern cursed himself for a fool and took the last six steps three at a time. Any sixth sense he might have felt owed was conspicuously absent. Heart hammering, he paused to catch his breath and let his eyes accommodate the murk, his gradually sharpening gaze scanning the grim interior.

The door to her apartment hung open, twisted back grotesquely against its shattered hinges. It made him think of the cheap funfair thrill rides of his teens.

With every new step he took, his hopes fell another notch.

The slaughterhouse stench was overpowering. The wooden stake in his hand felt heavy, reluctant. His mouth was dry and the comforting taste of bourbon was gone. He wanted to slip back downstairs and put his hand back under the driver's seat again. That want, and the charnel–house reek, made him feel like a trespasser in a mausoleum, a tomb raider and body thief.

"Don't be a fool," he hissed, pushing through the twisted splinters of wood and into Ashley Powell's apartment. Stake in one hand, claw hammer in the other. Ready.

Standing just beyond the threshold Stern noticed three things almost instantly. First, the reinforcement of the smell; the air laced with the ferrous taint of blood. Second, the stains, red streaks like elongated footprints dragged between the kitchen and the lounge. Third, the noise. Coming from inside the lounge. Someone struggling to rise, knocking something over as their hand flailed out. A grunt, half male, half female, neither sexless nor yet any single sex, the grunt becoming a scream, becoming a woman's scream...

He forced himself into taking another step. Four more to the door. He licked his lips. The hand clutching the stake was visibly shaking, the knuckles near white with the pressure. Still the wood felt slippery in his grip.

One step...

Stern eased himself forward, praying silently to whatever God would listen.

Two...

The smell was stronger now, still sickeningly fresh. The stains on the carpet would take some shifting. He nearly laughed out loud at the stupidity of that thought.

Three...

He stood level with the kitchen entrance, facing a thickening mosaic of blood that outlined the shape of a body. The body was gone. There were only haphazard gashes of blood left behind to streak the floor and walls. So much blood it couldn't all surely belong to the woman. Quietly, almost so quiet as to be silent, he heard the radio whispering out from the windowsill.

Even though it was close to being cold, Stern was sweating. Shifting the hammer to his left hand he wiped the right across his brow. God, he wanted a drink.

After, he promised himself.

Four...

He stepped around into the lounge doorway and saw the Christmas tree covered with its fine frosting of fake snow and its glitterballs reflecting miniature deaths in a thousand fragments across his eyes.

The woman was trying to stand. It was hard to see how she could, with so much blood leaking from her wounded flesh. Her legs were unsteady. She grabbed at the branches of the tree, brought the whole thing down on top of her.

Only then did he see the dead man, or rather the shell of the dead man lying on the floor, the face of St. Malachy's angel from his nightmares staring up blindly at the ceiling. The wooden stake slipped through his fingers.

She was alive, it, the thing, the Jesus Demon, was dead. It refused to lodge in his mind. He looked at the woman, saw her wounds, knew that if he didn't help she was going to bleed to death and soon. She lay there, her own eyes dancing with the shine of death approaching.

But he couldn't move.

GABRIEL was in the air when he felt her die.

A tall flaxen–haired stewardess was offering refreshments, whiskey and hot towels, her eyes a million miles away, hands moving in slow and listless motion, going through the motions, faking any feeling, when he began to vomit.

He coughed once and clutched at the back of the seat while she fumbled for the paper bag and tried to get it under his mouth. Another convulsion took him, arms folded across his stomach he doubled up in pain, his legs drawing up towards his chin. He put his hands up to his mouth as if trying to force it back into his stomach. The vomit just spilled through his fingers.

She pushed the bag beneath his face again, trying to coax him into its paper maw. It wasn't happening. Gabriel swallowed a lungful of sick–smelling air, tried to hold from vomiting again. Through the sickness an overwhelming sense of loss, of something simply ceasing to be, suffocated him, and an emptiness like blackness bit back, forcing its way out of his body this time as the hot wet rush of urine from his bladder and the stench of feces as his sphinter gave out in a sympathetic death as

The angel stepped forward...reached out...the rasp of agonized breaths...a sheen of blood clung with lover's intimacy to the thing's face, blood that washed all trace of humanity from its hating eyes...claws that should have been fingers pushed into her, gripped her, pulled her close so that the sting of the angel's overly–sweet breath brought tears to her eyes...and in that second it tasted the specter of Gabriel's presence...tasted his nearness and gazed not into her eyes but at the face reflected in them, back into its own eyes, and deeper, inside, into Gabriel's..."Do you want to live?"

he heard the angel's goading question echo inside his head, its voice drowning the stewardess's concern. He struggled to blank it out, stifle the angel's nearness but it was all he could do simply holding himself, the pain too wide and too deep. As he tried to hold himself together, Ashley's screams gave way to the smells of his emptied flesh as they corrupted everything trapped within the confines of the plane with their cloying reeks.

He looked at the stewardess, wanted to explain, but all she saw was a drunk who'd evacuated his stomach, bladder and bowels on her shift, her blind eyes didn't want to see, weren't prepared to see, the truth.

"Can I...can I...get cleaned up...somewhere?"

Disguised as tears, blood began to run from his eyes.

THE snow was falling thicker now, settling on the blacktop like creamy icing. Mannelli was alone in his old Toreno, chasing the headlights of Delgado's fishtailing Impala. Cigarette smoke played thickly with the trapped air, making ghosts out of the wispy tendrils of white. Outside, there was neither sun nor sky. He'd been here before, that was all he could think. He'd been behind the wheel of the same car, making the same desperate drive with a bunch of lemon yellow flowers forgotten on the passenger seat. Three years between the journeys, and no Gabriel with him this time, but the same stone–faced death waited at the end of both races.

Gabriel wasn't the only one with feelings.

The dispatcher's call had gone out for a 311, robbery in progress, and then he'd heard Ashley's address on the riverside.

"Please God let her be all right," he breathed, answering the call. All he could think of as his feet manipulated the pedals was the intense fear he'd heard in Gabriel's voice. Then, crossing himself: "Okay, I know I've probably used up my credits in the prayer department, God, but I'm kinda hoping you'll okay an overdraft just this once. Not for me you understand. For Gabriel." *You can't do this to him twice* he wanted to add, but of course God could do whatever He in His terrible wisdom wanted. Who was he, a second–generation lapsed Catholic, to argue?

Those eleven minutes, chasing through the maze of streets like a laboratory mouse, were the longest of Mannelli's life. He was exhausted and he was frightened. One feeling he was used to, could handle; the other he wasn't, and that made it all the more so. In front of him, Delgado took the last corner at a crawl, driving as if he were looking for a space in a supermarket parking lot.

Bill Stern's dusty blue Coupe was the first thing he saw as he turned onto Prospect.

Mannelli hit the breaks and the hazard blinkers simultaneously, cranking open the Torino's door and abandoning it in the middle of the road. He ran up the small rise of steps to Ashley's apartment building. The thick security door stood wedged open. It was wrong, it was all wrong, he wanted to argue with the cop in him but he knew instinctively it was right.

Swallowing down a mouthful of fear Mannelli drew his service .45 from its shoulder slung holster and forced himself to enter the foyer.

THE Angel of Red stretched out within the carapace of its new form, tasting the soft femine flesh against its singing nerve–endings, savoring the failing life juices of the newly dead as they melted into him, enjoying the desperate longing to live that lingered still.

He licked his tongue across her soft lips.

He felt the Color Dance swell around his–her–body, the driving hungers of the spectrum demanding another sacrifice but outside the dance, or maybe inside it, deeper inside within the swirl of negative and positive, dancing to the tramp of lightning and thunder, he felt them coming, closing in.

He'd seen the Indian's face in her dying eyes, looked out through the Indian's eyes and seen seats and people, and a woman. So beautiful, so, so beautiful as she had tried to help the Indian. He wanted to take her face in his hands and crush it. Feel the bone slowly give way. Feel the softness of her thoughts on his fingers as she stopped thinking forever.

Even as he felt his personality begin slipping away he dragged himself back to the present. The lights from the Christmas tree had gone out, a broken bulb somewhere in the chain, but with the tree upended on the floor and dirt spilling out of its pot it didn't matter that a bulb had stopped working.

The Angel turned slowly, sensing rather than hearing the newcomer with his arcane toys of superstition, his stake and his garlic. He–she–smiled at the sweat blistering the Watcher's pale, craggy face, at the intense relief burning in the pathetic man's eyes.

More footsteps were coming up the stairs. A long way down but running hard. More strength to them. Younger. Urgent. A real threat. Not like this wreck in front of him.

He–she–had to move quickly. Started screaming. Really screaming. And threw himself at the stunned man in the doorway, knocking the wooden stake from his hand, clawing at his face, and all the while screaming.

THE mixture of smells was incredible, disinfectant, ammonia, furniture polish and beneath them all, rising, death.

Climbing the stairs in a semi–darkness that lifted the higher he climbed, Mannelli made it around the second set of risers. The reason for the artifical brightness hung on broken hinges, Ashley's door and through it the light spilling in from the world.

Mannelli stopped moving. He felt cold all over, and despite the fact that he had run the scenario a thousand times through his head—both in the car and again charging up the twisting flights of stairs—he couldn't cross the threshold and make it all come true. It was a head–fuck. A rape of the soul that left him brittle.

"Sorry, Gabriel," he whispered, crossing himself. "I'm so sorry, Gabriel…" Behind him Delgado, Lambert and Kolchak started loudly up the stairs. Then she began screaming.

For a heartbeat, while he denied its reality, the door was closed and there were no screams. Everything was all right. But the door was open, could never be closed again, and he was moving with his gun suddenly feeling so very heavy in his hand. Weighing a life? More than a life, its gray metal suddenly weighing a death.

He stepped into a blood–smeared footprint. The carpet was gashed with haphazard splatters of blood, and each one of the staggered slashes of red dissolved another layer of hope that this might end in anything other than death, hers, his or someone else's. Hope ground like diamonds into dust in the palm of his hand. Mannelli caught sight of himself in the distant mirror as the screaming became unbearable. His finger curled around the snub–nosed .45's trigger pin.

Noises.

He couldn't separate them all at first.

Music beneath the screams. A man's grunts as flesh hit flesh beneath the music. Breathing…someone falling…

On the kitchen floor a dried pool of blood outlined the shape of a body. Though the body was gone, the stench lingered. Whoever it was had shit themselves as they died. The ugly truth of death. He ignored it all, followed the bloody stagger of footsteps into the lounge. In the light of the hall his worst fears merely simmered, hope taunting him with a deceitful hand held out for him to grasp at; but they began to boil as he crossed over into the slaughterhouse that had once been a lounge.

So much blood. So much blood. And the smell. Dear God, the smell.

And then the screaming snapped him into focus. A wreck of a body lay just beyond the door. Beyond salvation and therefore beyond a second look. In the center of the room Bill Stern hunched over Ashley's body. The claw hammer in his right hand was raised to strike.

"Hold it right there, motherfucker!" Mannelli screamed, bringing the .45 up and pulling the trigger in a single smooth pull. He didn't have time to aim or pray. It was either going through Stern's head, his hand, thin air or Ashley.

The bullet slammed into Stern's hand, opening his fingers and sending the hammer spinning.

Stern's head tilted as the scream was torn from his lips. Behind him Ashley whimpered.

Unable to believe the truth of his ears, Mannelli thumbed back the hammer on the .45 and cleared his throat. He heard Delgado coming through the door. No second chances. "Turn around, Bill. It's over." He didn't hear his own words. As Stern turned to face him, he pulled the trigger sending a single bullet into Bill Stern's surprised face and making his obese body pirouette into the oblivious arms of death. The sound of the shot was deafening. Stern slumped forward, the sound of his fall loud in the silence following the gunshot.

Tears streaming down his cheeks, Daniel Mannelli walked over to the body of his surrogate father, kicked it over with his foot and pumped five more rounds into the dead man's head.

seventy nine

JACK Delgado froze in the doorway, counting the shots.

One...

A pause.

Two, three, four, five, six in rapid succession followed by a desolate banshee–like wail.

Delgado looked right, into the kitchen, taking in the wide pool of drying blood. And left, into the lounge. There was a heavy smell in the room; the stench of an ugly death, a bloater–floater or a shallow grave. He had to breathe but it was difficult to expel the fetid air from his lungs, impossible to shift the taste it left behind in his mouth. Delgado saw Mannelli first, cradling the head of a woman in his lap. Blood matted in the thick bangs of hair. Some of it hers but more of it belonging to the two dead bodies that shared the room with them. Mannelli was weeping, rocking to and fro on his knees, not looking at the woman he was cradling. He brushed a strand of blood clotted hair from her too–white forehead. She was crying too, softly but without tears.

Delgado's eyes swept the room quickly. Two bodies, one gutted like a fish while the head of the other one was made unrecognizable by the opalescent coating of blood and the pulverized mesh of bullet wounds covering it but the body, the clothing, was familiar. Too familiar. A friend lying dead. Another friend wrecked because of it. Delgado looked at Lambert and Kolchak.

Lambert was looking down at the torn and mutilated body of Carlos Lamenzo, a garland of bloody tears around its open ribcage. An instant later sickness knifed his stomach. But that was it, it came and it went and he was the street–hardened cop again.

"Looks like we've got The Trinity," he said.

"Sure does," Delgado agreed bitterly, thinking of the days Bill Stern had stood by his side, friends, partners. Something had pushed him this way, guys like Stern didn't suddenly wake up one morning as dysfunctional sociopaths. Something had broken him. Jack Delgado looked down at the body of the man who he had once been proud to call his friend. He owed him that much, one last look as a friend before Stern became the monster the world was going to make him. Things, simple things, stopped making sense.

Kolchak had never seen anything like it in his life. In the kitchen behind them, bent double, he vomited into the sink.

"Let's get them covered up and him out of here." Him could have been Kolchak or Mannelli. Then: "It's over, Dan," he said softly, laying a hand on Mannelli's shoulder. "You didn't have a choice. You really didn't."

"Why, Jack?" Mannelli asked, looking up with the wounds of betrayal in his eyes. "Why?"

eighty

THE Angel lay in his arms, letting the weeping man stroke his—her—hair and play protector while the police secured the crime scene. It was a pitiful sham. They photographed the bodies from every angle, covered them, talked quietly about one of their own gone bad.

It was too easy to smile, to let his lips curl into satisfaction, when he—she—was supposed to be the victim here. The helpless woman needing the big strong protectors. But the smile was there, inside, when he looked at the mess of The Watcher's face and saw another aspect of his dark secret dying with those six bullets.

Now only one of the wraiths from St. Malachy's still walked this land of the would—be dead, Gabriel Rush, the Little Indian Boy, and he (at least some part of him) was inside this shell with the Angel. Inside the dead flesh of his love, memories and weaknesses to be trawled while the Angel sought the means of his undoing.

He allowed them to help him—her—stand and be ushered towards the door and the cars waiting in the street below. Said: "Gabriel..."

"He's on his way home, Ashley. On a plane now."

"Yes," he said, tasting the rightness of it. On his way back into New York City, back into his glassy territory. There would be more blood. He could feel the song singing in his veins. One more sacrifice and then the dance could truly begin.

"We're going to get you to a hospital. Get you checked out," The olive skinned policeman said soothingly. "But everything's going to be okay now. It's over. I promise."

Ah, the Angel savored the already broken promise, wondered why these humans were compelled to promise what they couldn't deliver.

"Yes..." he—she—said again, picturing the face of the last dead man walking back into his cold embrace. "Gabriel."

It was almost time. Almost time.

GABRIEL left the 747 with his clothes in a clear poly-thene bag, borrowed loose-fitting, pleated slacks and a white cotton shirt, his only protection from the cold. The sky above his head was the red of a lost battle, dawn rising. He felt the sting of tears on his cheeks, not his, the wind's. A fresh layer of virgin snow blanketed the taxi rank and the roads out of JFK. The only place he could think of going was home, but without Ashley there to hold him he did-n't think it could ever be home again. A simple word like *home* had somehow become the hot tip of a nee-dle ready to slip into tongue even before the sounds had begun to leave his mouth.

He thought again about the killer. Wanted to turn to the girl standing in the taxi rank smelling of Ashley's perfume and say: "I feel so alone. Can you understand that? He killed her. Cut my soul out." But he didn't say anything. He thought about calling Mannelli to hear what he already knew. Getting it second hand would make it all the more real.

Gabriel walked towards the crossing, stopping beneath the hazy ghost–like glow of the DON'T WALK sign. Across the road, against the glare of neon, a man was silhouetted blue, there but not there, not really. He recognized the man wrapped in shim-mering Harmony. Knew he was on the other side, not just of the road, he knew that he was dead.

Gabriel closed his eyes and opened them again. Bill Stern hadn't moved.

HE leaned his weight against the lamppost, unable to feel its solidity and happy at last to be away from it all. There were tears in his eyes, copper–colored tears of blood that mingled with the six craters burned into his face by the gun. The Watcher was glad he couldn't see himself. Glad for the protection of the slowly falling snow. For the cloak of invisibility it draped across his broad shoulders.

He was The Watcher Eternal.

He had Harmony.

What more could he want?

I too have spoken with the dead, he whispered in a voice no one could hear, *and they tell me this life is a fine place to be.*

He could want that; he could want life.

Gabriel Rush waited on the other side, his feet bringing him across the black tar of the road. It isn't over, he tried to say, but nothing came out. No warning for the last of them. No warning for the wraiths of St. Malachy's. Only then did he understand. He was alone. The Watcher Eternal, on a street corner, alone. Bitter and ironic, that was the taste of Harmony.

THE ghost of the dead girl walked away from the hospital ward as the rain began to fall.

The medics had flapped and flustered, wanting to run their checks, their CT Scans and their Chem 7's but she had brushed them off, like the survivor of an auto wreck on the Tappan Zee, she'd walked out of the ward, drinking in the twin aromas of ammonia and detergent. The caustic smells burned her eyes, but that didn't matter. In the glass of a fire door she stared at herself, liking what she saw.

No wonder the Little Indian Boy enjoyed his woman. She was delicious. Her heart beat faster as she touched the soft skin around her eyes, trying it on for size, moving the tendon beneath as if her skin were stretched over a colony of worms.

"Come to me, my dear one, come find me and we'll dance the final dance...I'll be waiting where it all began. I'll be waiting."

The door swung closed behind her, in the distance the alarm sounded as another soul crashed. She walked away in her borrowed skirt to the music death, her feet taking her towards the gabled roof of St. Malachy's.

eighty four

A part of Gabriel wanted to grab up a broken stone from the roadside and hurl it at Stern's shade, but what was the point? Where was the justice when a man could lose all he loved not once but twice?

Instead, he said a prayer for the dead man and went back to his empty apartment above the laundry just outside of Chinatown to sink down amongst the photographs of everything he had lost. It was strange, walking around the apartment, just how much of Ashley had snuck into his life, simple things like shampoo in the bathroom, her ladyshave on the side of the tub, lipstick and gloss on the nightstand, underwear in the dirty linen. Even her handwriting on the shopping list stuck to the fridge. Little bits of her had found their way into all of his secret places, places that weren't meant to be shared, even with loved ones. It wasn't going to be a case of finding reminders of her for days or weeks or even months, things that were going to make him break down were going to be there forever, her essence was so deeply immersed in the four walls of his life that Gabriel was going to be running into the ghosts of her for as long as he could keep running, and even if time made him stronger, nothing could make him forget. And the ghosts? They might fade but they would never truly disappear.

They might be cast back in the reflections of the lingerie store window on 5th Avenue, or echo from the walls of the pancake place on West 48th. They might walk beside him through Prospect Park, slipping an ethereal hand into his, simply content to walk and watch the sun go down. They might tut quietly at the sight of a parent pulling at a child in the supermarket line or whistle at the 4th of July fireworks lighting the sky.

Aimee Mann suited his mood, so Gabriel rolled himself a cigarette and sat back with nothing but the music going on. It lasted less than two songs, then he felt it pulling at him, a darkness on the edge of his consciousness, goading with the sweet voice of Ash…

Come to me, my dear one, come find me and we'll dance the final dance…I'll be waiting where it all began. I'll be waiting.

"You win," he said out loud. "I don't have the strength." And that was the truth, there was only so much strength inside any man and this one was stretched thin.

But still, five minutes later Gabriel was standing on the sidewalk, steam venting from the grille at his feet. He mingled with the jaywalkers too impatient to wait for the WALK sign crossing into Canal Street and heading north, passed the discount jeans stores and the exotic delis, the windows full of fake watches and the cut–price walkmans.

The city was awash with noise and scents, shrimps hissing on the hot plates, barkers calling out the daily news, the chorus of car horns playing the crosstown jam. Someone humming Springsteen's Thunder Road beneath their breath. The war vet with his amputated leg resting on the sidewalk outside of the diner. All the familiar idiosyncrasies of his beloved Manhattan, and yet it was all so very different right then. It was as if he were seeing the world through new eyes; the eyes of an angel.

There was no blinding flash of light, no God–like clapping of thunderous noise. Instead, from fingertips to the roots of his hair, Gabriel felt a mild electrical tingling as if some primal untapped instinct was slowly waking. With it came a sense of calmness. Ease. Walking past the huge plate–glass window of Barnes & Noble he felt the tension begin to ebb from his tightly coiled muscles. And that was when he was hit by the betrayal:

Hanging by the neck from a streetlamp, a small black–skinned boy, eyes eaten through by the insects swarming over his corpse. *Die Nigger Die!* had been sprayed across his small chest in red paint. It was difficult to read for the blood.

Gabriel reeled backwards, ears filled with laughing and jeering crescendo of chittering insect–voices. The sudden force of the movement had him staggering into the path of a briskly walking suit and briefcase and stumbling a few steps before his legs finally gave way beneath him.

The need to vomit clogged up in his throat but the horror was gone. There was no child hanging from the lamppost. He dragged himself up to his knees.

"Now you see what I see, live with what I live with, my Little Indian Chief," the angel hissed inside his head. "He died there, a month, a year ago, it doesn't matter, he's always there for me. I'll never forget him and neither will you…"

"Get. Out. Of. My. Head!" Gabriel hissed, slamming the heels of his hands into his temples. He knew people were staring at him hunched there on his knees, balled fists pressed into the sides of his skull, people walking along in the comfort of their nice, normal, mundane lives.

"Just another part of the freakshow, that's what they think you are," the Angel of Red taunted. "Another one of the inmates escaped the Asylum. Welcome to MY world."

And suddenly the secrets from those mundane lives were humming inside Gabriel's head, first as whispers:

"Yes, I think I love her."

"Lets make it real, lets do it..."

"Fuck you, bitch!"

"I didn't promise you heaven..."

"Whore."

"Bastard."

And then louder, secrets spilling in the voices of Manhattan until he was drowning in the city's secret life:

"Lets cut a deal, okay," one hissed.

"This is my woman, nigger," another threatened, steel in its tone.

"Didn't I tell you?"

"Moron."

"Fuckwit."

"Get outta my face..."

"Jesus Christ, what does Moreno think he's doing with that cunt? She's young enough to be his granddaughter."

"I said kiss my lillywhite ass..."

"I didn't mean to hurt you, honey..."

"I said don't fuckin' move or I'll cut you up so bad..."

"She was pregnant..."

"White meat..."

"I didn't mean to..."

"Pushed her down the stairs...I stood behind her and pushed... I pushed her..."

"I miss you, angel..."

"You fucked her? You fucking well fucked her? You fucker..."

Gabriel's face twisted, the pain of three million lives swelling inside his brain, clamoring to get in deeper. Each voice with its own anguished tale to tell. Its own tragedies to whisper straight into his soul: Abuse, molestations and muggings, love, death, needles and rinds, highs and lows, blockers and poppers, beatings and burglaries, alcohol and separation, divorce and custody battles, betrayal and forgiveness...

Every voice was a victim, every word an avenue into a street of pain. It took everything Gabriel had just to raise his head from the cracked sidewalk.

"Leave me alone," he begged the angel inside him.

"Leave you alone," it mocked. "But, my Little Indian, why should I?"

"Please..." it was a whimper forced between clenched teeth.

"I haven't even begun."

The spiderweb of cracks broken through paving slab beneath his hands began, slowly, to leak color. They bled like veins of mingled reds, deep red through rust to rose, the residue leaking out into the street thick enough to actually be blood. As it bled across his fingers Gabriel felt a surge of hatred for the angel sharing his head, that surge feeding off the stolen memory of Ashley's screams fading, her face kissing the softness of the carpet. Of her struggling desperately to rise, already undone by weakness, by the promise of nevermore, flowing through her veins...trying to talk as the life leaked out of her...and for a second, a fragment of a second, Gabriel understood. Tasted the intensity of emotion burning through his soul, and understood everything the angel offered.

It would have been easy, so easy to give himself over to it; he would have, but for the feathered angel of Mott Street, a starling whose wings dripped the serene blue of flight as it flittered over the newspaper vendor's stall.

That glimpse of harmony was enough to jar Gabriel. Make him realize that the pure red anger singing through his veins wasn't his own. In that icy moment of clarity the starling swooped from the air to the litter–strewn gutter, the essence dripping from its wings shot through with streaks of black, as black as night itself. Gabriel watched it feed on the dead rat, the secret geography of death illuminated by the shifting dance of colors that bathed the starling's body in light.

"Death," the voice inside his head crooned, "the black, is as vital as dreaming."

There were thoughts in Gabriel's head, images, pictures and words that belonged to the angel, that offered a chance at understanding what it already knew. The secrets.

The tide of Colors lapped at Gabriel's body, like the rising tide threatening to bring down a lonely sandcastle. Gabriel watched it all, entranced by the harlequin Dance of Color that was life, the greens and the golds, the blues, the spectrum so perfectly balanced that all feelings could coexist, but not so entranced that he couldn't sense the nearness of death.

It was like looking at the same old streets, the same old world, but seeing them with new eyes.

The Land of Colored Glass.

Gabriel pushed himself to his feet, needing the support of the streetlight to keep standing. People passed on all sides, carrying with them their own coats of many colors. The whole street was a brilliant, impossible canvas exploding to life all around him. But it was a thing canvas. A fragile one. Built of colored glass. People with their own haloes clustered together according to their colorations as if some optical magnetism was at work, drawing like to like.

He stood look a man in a tidal wave of color, being buffetted and bullied by ranks of gray shuffling by, a spray of yellow so vibrant it could have been a scattering of doubloons along Main Street. And every third or fourth wave, a jumble of pure randomness would wend its way past, reveling in the disparities of emotion and character. Gabriel simply soaked it up, mouthful after drunken mouthful, like a blind man cursed with the gift of sight.

From behind him, down the street, he heard a scream. And laughter.

The laughter taken up by the thing inside his head.

Around him, the street dissolved into a muddy wash of red. Amid the dissolution of color, a pregnant woman lay on the floor, clutching at her belly. She was sobbing, trying desperately to protect the baby inside her whilst a skeletally tall teenager blazing red like an inferno leveled kick after hate–filled kick at her. Then he was sprinting off towards the subway entrance with her bag in his hands.

It was all over so quickly. Yet nobody moved to help the woman until her attacker had disappeared down through the hole in the ground.

He smelled the sweet scent of cinnamon drifting out of a Starbucks' doorway carrying with it the truth; life goes on…

THE Angel of Red stared at the twisting spire of St. Malachy's as it rose up before her stolen feet. A great stone monster obsessed with the Immaculate Conception. Her nostrils flared, scenting the last of the witnesses on the wind. Back where it all began. The smile on her face spoke of the ecstasy shuddering through her body, each tremor a new, sheer delight, as phantom bullets slammed into her. She gasped her pleasure, as near to pure undiluted and erotically charged sex as this body had ever felt, reliving the death dance of Carlos Lamenzo not twenty feet from where she stood now.

A drunk sat huddled between the graves, the synapses of his addled mind singing with the lies of the unholy communion–blood wrapped protectively in his brown paper bag.

"Welcome to my world," she crooned, laughing at the drunk as he struggled to stand. Her world was gradually filming over with a patina of red glass supple enough for each stem of grass to ripple with the caress of the choked inner city breeze. The failing light left the stars looking like dewdrops spattered on velvet and the old church like the little plastic castle at the bottom of a goldfish bowl. Around her the bushes and trees took on the haunting aspect of crucified scarecrows as the skin of red enveloped them, making each trunk, each branch into another skeletal limb. All around, the churchyard branches sparkled against the halo of the twilight sun, catching and reflecting the whole spectrum of colors yet somehow radiating a pure, blazing red, strong enough to fill the whole city with its hate.

The church was all angles and pillars, windows pointing like accusing fingers at the darkening sky. The dressed stone had grayed with exhaust fumes and the tragedy of everyday life but still St. Malachy's looked magnificent in its gothic splendor. Every angle so precise, roses carved into the body of the pillars, florets and coronets atop them. Two hundred and eighty feet to the stone cross capping the belltower and still St. Malachy's was an anachronism dwarfed by skyscrapers of glass and steel that stretched five times her height. Out of place and out of time.

The Angel of Red smiled herself a hateful smile, captivated by the work of God, amused that it lay so utterly bereft of life; a playground of junkies, drunks and whores. She walked slowly, still adjusting to the quirks of her borrowed body, and placed her hands out flat on the cold stone as if feeling for a pulse. The old stones were as dead as their deity.

A shiver of pleasure shuddered through Ashley Powell's body, the physical memory of a bullet bursting through Carlos Lamenzo's spinal cord. Beneath her hands a film of resinous red glass melted over the stone. She lifted her hand higher. The sticky glass began to flow up the wall, trying to reach her fingers. Smiling, the angel began a slow spiderclimb up the face of the old church, one hand at a time, the glass film working like glue to hold her slight weight as she ventured higher. Every foot gained drew the veil of red glass higher until it began to obscure the beauty of the old religion with the malice of the new.

Manhattan spread out beneath her eyes, gray and labyrinthine like so many twists and turns of the laboratory maze, all leading back to St. Malachy's. Did they know this when they built the old church? That it bisected all angles of the city so equilaterally? The streets could have been brightly colored ribbons where neon signs and car headlights joined with the secret underlife of colors. Her fingers dug through the safety of the glass film into the hardness of the wall, flaking stone.

Where to look? Where was her Little Indian Boy?

The Angel of Red's nostrils flared, trying to catch Gabriel Rush's scent on the swirling winds. He was out there...close...

A flurry of wind gusted around her, curling around the church's conical spire, plucking at her clothes like a demanding child as she scuttled upwards, reaching for the small stone cross that marked the summit. With all the irony of an angelic rodeo rider, the glass angel straddled the cross as if it was some beast waiting to be tamed. From its perch up on the cross the mesh of multi–colored lines dissecting the city might have been some kind of intricate electrical diagram, wires connecting each and every home and life down there. But the angel knew them for what they were, the lullaby of life, harmony and tranquility, hatred and vengeance, sung by the streets on a failing winter night.

The angel closed her eyes, savoring the moment, the snatches of the song of life, even as she sensed him. The one white light in the city. The one light that shone brighter than the rest. She didn't need to open her eyes to see him. Gabriel Rush was this one dazzling white nimbus cutting through the falling night like a blade cleaving through Manhattan's idiot heart.

The angel licked a dry tongue across Ashley's sandpaper lips, following the gossamer strands of light with its eyes, tracing them from the sea of souls all the way back to the doors of St. Malachy's.

"Come to me, beauty," she crooned in her stolen voice.

"Get out of my head," Gabriel begged, clutching at his temples in an attempt to drive the demons out of his skull.

He was staggering down the sidewalk like a drunk, stumbling into things, a woman sluicing down the steps of her tenement block with a hose, a Popeye–like man overloaded with one–liter Coke bottles on his way to the recycling bins, a three–legged dog and one of the war veterans on his board panhandling outside a downtown music store. They just pushed him away, sent him staggering further down the street no different from any other drunk or crazy. No one stopped to help him, but why would they? All they saw was a lunatic clutching at his temples, almost pulling his hair out and babbling about voices inside his head.

On the corner of Cicero, Gabriel fell to his knees, driven down by the sheer assault of voices, personalities opening themselves up to him. Battered on every side by the hopes and dreams of Manhattan as they coiled about him, blanketed him with a terrible, bleak desperation that smothered him. He didn't have the strength to shut them out, all of their pains and petty thoughts drowning his own personality beneath their crude waves of passion. The maelstrom of emotions threatened to overwhelm him completely if he couldn't throw up some form of defense against the consciousness of everyone around him. Barricade his soul from all of the hatred humming in the air. Barricade it from the underworld of appetite and hunger that made the real one turn.

The assault was so fierce he barely noticed the rest of the world, the solid, tangible world, as it passed by the corner of his dilated eye. Gabriel groped out, looking for something to support him as he struggled to stand again. His hand closed on a restless coil of shifting light. The thing was like some huge snake...no, an umbilical cord, stretching impossibly back to the earth mother. His head span with wonderment whilst his eyes feasted on the snake of life in his hands, awed, hungry, and afraid as to why the miracles were coming apart.

The pains of Manhattan were nothing next to the hatred spiraling inside Gabriel. It was as if a red mist had smothered his eyes. The world was coming undone and the hatred blazing inside him was just one small way in which the nuts and bolts of humanity were loosening. He cast about desperately looking for something to vent that hatred on, something to batter until the agony in his fists was loud enough to silence the voices crying out in his head. Something to punch, to hit, to kick, with all of the anger, all of the hate, that was knotted up inside him until it bled out of him. Until it dripped red on the sidewalk. Until it hardened like rust on the walls. Until it seeped into the very fabric of the city itself...

The auras of people treading the drab, gray streets where the snow had melted to slush held firm for the moment, but for how much longer? How long would it take for all of those hatreds to seep into the streets and the buildings? How much longer would it take to have fissures cracking through the skyscrapers, red mouths opening in the sides of Wall Street and Broadway with sharp–edged teeth ready to eat–

Gabriel shook his head, trying to force the alien thoughts out and some how reign down on the tidal swell of emotions churning around inside him. "The madness will pass," he whispered, framing Ashley's face in his Mind's Eye. If he could only shut it out, or isolate it, he would be okay. In response:

"Look upward, my little Hiawatha..." the angel within mocked.

Across the street, back where it all began, where Gabriel had stumbled onto a miracle in the guise of a child killer being gunned down by New York's finest, towered the brooding edifice of St. Malachy's.

"I hate you."

The church's maudlin spire drew his traitorous eyes. It was like gazing upon a finely cut chalice and seeing his own reflection manufactured a thousand thousand times in its cuts and angles, and in each reflection his eyes were accusing, the darkness within them whispering his fear.

"I've killed you once," he breathed aloud, trying to mask his own voice clamoring inside his mind, the one obsessed with the truth: "I'm scared... I don't want to die..."

"Oh, have you? I don't feel very dead..."

Gabriel made it as far as the white line cutting through the road before the relentless waves of hatred coming off the old church stopped him in his tracks. They were physical. As physical as any gale. Strong enough to drive him back a staggered step.

"Frightened of me?" he hissed between clenched teeth, pushing himself on even as the skin stretched taut across his cheeks and the muscles in his face began to twitch and vibrate, coming alive like maggots beneath the thin reality of his flesh. With each step it felt as if his eyes would rupture and ooze blind jelly, the winds of hate like a knife delivering one lethal wound after another. And then, suddenly, the knives were real. The huge stained glass windows beneath the spire shattered outwards as if mere glass couldn't contain all of the hatred that was bottled up within those four walls. Splinters of multi–colored glass sprayed out across the street, cutting into him. Gabriel turned his face away from the ragged glass as it rained down on him. Each splinter and shard biting where it fell.

When Gabriel looked back, a film of red glass had sealed the wound in St. Malachy's facade. He walked through the litter of broken glass that lay ignored and glittering on the floor, his gaze raised to the fire blazing redly where the cross should have been.

The vaulted roof and the stretching spire of blood red glass caught the darkness of the sun and the night together and threw it back at the sky. A glass tower coruscating against a scarlet sky. A magnificent red beacon to all of the evils mankind's twisted minds could imagine.

"How do you kill an angel?"

Inside the heart of the church somewhere, a crack, like timbers breaking.

The corpse of a woman came staggering through the bronze doors of the nave, smoke chasing after her. Her thick winter coat crackled and burned, the sparks igniting her long dark hair even as she swatted at her head trying to beat the flames out. Gabriel couldn't move; tried to tell himself she was dead already. That there was nothing he could do. She opened her mouth to scream but no sounds made it out of the mess that was her throat. Wisps of smoke curled around her lips. Lingered on her teeth as if they wanted one last kiss, one last nibble before the said goodbye.

It took Gabriel a moment to realize there were no flames burning away in the building behind her and understand that it was the intimate glass skin that hugged her body like cellophane that had ignited, that it was the very hate of the woman herself that consumed her. That she truly burned with hatred.

She fell to her knees, flame–wreathed arms beating ineffectually at her sides as the fire ate her once–pretty face, her hands like fiery batons conducting her own death until she pitched forward. Her husk lay smoldering on the sidewalk until it had burned out. Even with the flames gone, the stench of charred flesh clung to the air with its taint.

Gabriel stood there, mesmerized by the human torch, the angel's last taunting question ringing in his ears…

How do you kill an angel?

eighty seven

SILVER bullet? Crucifix? A stake through the heart?

All of the legends invented by the old horror movies ran through his mind as he stepped into the nave. It was as if he had walked into a meat locker, sub–zero air frosting on the stone floor, the perfect rime broken only by the pale ghosts of the dead woman's footsteps where they staggered up the aisle. He scratched at the bird tattooed on his chest. Nothing had changed. Despite all of the miracles, all of the impossibilites that had been spawned and spun away crazily after that first bullet took Carlos Lamenzo's life, nothing inside this old stone relic had changed. The cool vault of the old church still smelled of myrrh and spikenard and the slightly sweet aroma of burning votive candles. Shadows painted the holy trinity on the floor.

Gabriel walked slowly down the aisle, walking in the dead woman's footsteps passed the guttering candles lined up against the wall, drawn towards the narthex, by the memory of –

seeing him rise, the Resurrection Man pull himself to his feet, the circle of men gathered in the church fired. Nine guns. Nine new deaths struck him: upper thigh, groin, abdomen, cheek, spleen, lungs, heart, and arm. The boy in the middle danced to the push and shove of the bullets but somehow managed to go on living and haul himself to his feet. Another gun fired again, launching a second volley of fire. Two shots took him in the chest, one ploughed through his temple, another into his leg, four went wide.

"Look at me," the angel on the floor said as it drew itself erect…it reached out to take the Resurrection Man by the hand…"A life for a life… I've waited a long time, do you want to live?"

"Do I want to?" the boy, bleeding from the wounds driven into his corpse, asked himself. There was only one answer: "Yes…"

—No Face Jesus stepping down from the crucifix above the altar and breathing life into Carlos Lamenzo's corpse.

The sun's light had faded some of the wound left in the crucifixion scene by the wooden Jesus' fall from grace, but the gash left behind was still raw, as if someone had stolen the moon from the sky and tried to color in the hole with a black crayon. Another testament to the reality of the miracle. They really had seen a dead man walk that day.

It was a lie, of course, to pretend that nothing had changed. There was no Father D'Angelo leaning against the sanctuary rail mumbling a useless prayer as Gabriel walked down the aisle. The people had changed: Francesca, Sam, Ashley.

Gabriel stepped over the low railing and reached for the door to the belltower. His hands twitched uselessly for want of some kind of weapon, the comfort of a talisman, useless or not, something outside of him, solid and real, that he could draw strength from. As it was, he was alone as he began the long climb towards death. Outside, it was raining. The raindrops loud on the rooftop.

"Come to me, my little Indian...I want to taste your soul."

GABRIEL took a deep breath, the fingers of his right hand clawing at the itchy raven tattooed on his chest. The edges of the painted bird burned. His skin crawled. The combination of sensations made it feel as if the black bird were struggling to fly free of his body, hungry for a life of its own.

He felt sickness rising in his craw.

It wasn't the claustrophobic stairway or the height. It was fear. Fear like an illness sweeping through his system. He felt lightheaded, dizzy. Part of him felt less real somehow. As if he had already passed over into the land of dead souls. His body was on the edge of betraying him as he reached out for the brass handle that would open the timber door to the church roof. He was shaking. The stone steps beneath his feet gently rocking like the sea lapping at the shore, threatening to tip him all the way back down to earth.

He wasn't ready but it didn't matter. Nothing he could have done would have been able to prepare him for what waited on the other side of the door.

ASHLEY stood on the watershed of the gently gabled roof, a ghost framed by the too–bright streetlights and the tired moon. She could have been an angel but for the blue–black bruises around her eyes and the strangulation wounds around her neck. She looked as if she'd been beaten or hadn't slept in days. Her hair dripped water into her eyes. She stood there, a dead girl crying rain as she held her hands out to him.

"Help me, Gabriel," she said. The wind played with her soaked skirt, pressing the thin floral print material up against her legs, building an illusion as it flowed around her. She looked helpless...innocent in a way she never had...

Gabriel picked at his chest, seeking some kind of reassurance from the wise bird, but the tattooed raven was real and it told him one thing: eyes lie.

Still, he couldn't find the words in him to deny the hope that somehow it could be her.

Worm Pipe, the thought was in his head but he didn't know if it was his own...so many years ago Wind Runner had sat him on his knee before the campfire and woven the legend of Worm Pipe, the husband who, so much in love with his new bride that he couldn't let her die, travelled to the Ghost Lodge in the Land of Dead Souls and begged for her life from his ancestors ghosts. He brought her back...but that was just a story...there was no Ghost Lodge...no Sky River...no Earth Mother...they were all stories, just like Napi, the First Father...

"Ash," Gabriel breathed, trying to grasp the truth somewhere from within the need to believe the miracle standing before him. "I thought...I thought." He thought he had seen her die, through her own eyes and then, twisted about, through the eyes of her killer, but how could he say that?

Ashley made an uncertain step towards him.

She had something in her hand. It took him a moment to realize what it was: a wilted rose. It was as if she had reached out and slammed her fist, dead flower and all, into his gut. He staggered back beneath the weight of the vision of another girl with a rose–

A sad faced girl alone in a street corner bar, drinking her day away. Between her fingers she twirled a flawed rose. Delicate white petals flaunting their imperfection; a single red tear weeping through the silk weave. There was something desperate in the way her long, sculptured fingernails pinched the fake stem. Her gaze drifted out of the window, to the lamppost across the wide street, some ghost of her past leaning against it, watching her.

Through the lens she looked less an angel, more a dead dreamer only anchored to this earth by the weight of her thoughts.

–Gabriel had put flowers on her grave the day he'd visited Sam.

He shook his head. "No." It was barely a word. A denial. He was reaching inside his jacket for the snubnosed .38, not caring that it wasn't loaded with silver bullets, that he had no prayer for the dying angel. It felt heavy in his hand, but not heavy enough. How heavy should a life be? Heavier than a gun, surely. Heavier than the bullet that kills. "You're not Ashley…" was all he said as he leveled the pistol's hungry black eye on the body of his love.

He couldn't hold his aim. It was the hardest thing he had ever done. Holding a gun on the woman he loved. His finger tightened around the trigger but the gun refused to hold still, to keep its aim.

He heard her laughing inside his head and was sure that he had finally slipped into the mouth of madness.

Her eyes are empty, he told himself, her eyes are empty…it's not her, not my Ash…

Gabriel wanted to believe he saw a flicker of Ashley in those eyes, but whilst she might have spoken with Ashley's voice, the difference was in her eyes. Ashley was gone. Still, he wanted it to be Ashley as he brought the .38 back up to lock eyes with his dead lover. Wanted her to understand, to know what it cost to pull the trigger.

"I won't forget to put roses on your grave," he whispered, closing his eyes as he squeezed the trigger. He couldn't bear to see.

The sound of the gunshot was deafening.

And after it, for a long second, there was only the sound of the rain drumming on the old church's roof.

Rain.

And inside:

Pain.

GABRIEL opened his eyes to see—

...a sad–faced man with tired raven–black hair that touched his shoulders aiming a gun at him...the man's almost red skin was wet with the rain...the scar beneath his left eye twitching to the tiny tremors beneath his cheek...his hand was shaking...the gun came up again...the black eye of the barrel wider and blacker than the doorway gaping behind this would–be killer...

He tried desperately to move his arms, his legs, but they refused...he watched helplessly as three more bullets hit, one stealing the sight from his eyes as it exploded in the tissue behind the socket, bathing the world in red...blood...one shattering his knee, betraying his balance on the rain–slick roof...the last one slamming into his chest...pushing him back...too far...he felt the world begin to tilt...the roof beneath his feet treacherous, like glass...

"How do you kill an angel," a voice inside his head mocked, taking all the burning, all the pain...absorbing it...living through it...but there was something else under it...another emotion...stronger than all the hate in the world...

It came for him then, scrambing across the treacherous rooftop, claws hungry for his heart. There was nothing of Ashley in it. The thing scrabbling across the roof was pure beast.

"You don't," Gabriel said aloud, pulling himself back before the Angel of Red's fear overwhelmed him. "Angels fall." He fired again, the last bullet. This time he didn't aim at the angel in Ashley's skin, but at the ground beneath her feet. The tile fractured. It very nearly didn't break but the Angel's weight was too much. Ashley teetered dangerously as the roof betrayed her. Her hand clawed helplessly at the air, trying to grab something to hold on to as another tile broke. And one next to it. They tumbled like dominoes as the Angel flapped around trying to save itself. But there was no salvation to be found on a church roof in the dark heart of winter. Only death.

"We're not the same," Gabriel said softly, in answer to all of the taunts the Angel had planted in his head. "We're not even similar..."

In one last desperate lunge of anger, it threw itself at Gabriel, fingernails so close to raking across his chest, stinging blood. The sound of his blood, his heart, beat loud in its ears as the Angel fell to the roof on all fours, snapping its jaws and snarling like some animal gone feral.

Gabriel didn't so much as flinch. "Kill me then," he whispered, thinking of Frankie, Sam, Ash. Everything he had lost. He lowered the gun to his side, waiting, praying silently for the death blow that would bring them all together...

In the belltower high above, the old bells began to peel with a multitude of voices, heavenly and angelic, desperate and demonic. With each chime another tile shattered like glass beneath the falling Angel's weight.

It understood. Next to the hunger, the need to silence the last witness, there was real fear in Ashley's ruined eyes. There was a crack. Something deep and terminal breaking within the roof's timbers.

"Do you want to live?" it hissed inside Gabriel's head as if it hadn't heard him.

"No," Gabriel said simply, holding the Angels' gaze as its face blurred into those of his friends, a gallery of guilt owned by one man...Bill Stern, Jay Bogdanovich, Seth Lawson, Al Culpepper, Jackson Carlisle, a sad–faced Celine—Charlotte—Annuci, the flower girl with her stained rose, Father Joe on a mattress in a bed-sit, and the last mask, the one that lingered, refusing to fade, Ashley. The future..."I've already lost everything worth living for..."

A splinter. Another crack. A scream of wood.

The Angel's fingers clawed at the collapsing roof. The feral hunger that had immolated in its eyes a moment before dulled, and a deep blue–green sea swelled in its place as the timbers and tiles beneath it finally sundered and fell inwards. Ashley's hand came up, reaching out, and then she was gone, torn away by the fall.

Gabriel closed his eyes. It was over. Where his story started, it ended, full circle. He wanted to cry but there were no tears left inside, only emptiness where so many people had been.

THE tolling of the bells slowed, became funereal, playing out a song of mourning.

With each lonely chime a shifting, ghostly figure began to take shape within the sanctuary of St. Malachy's, each born of a color, each part of a brilliant, impossible, glassy rainbow of life conjured to circle the dead body on the floor.

An ageless body, an angel to some, wreathed in white, knelt by the corpse of its fallen brother, it's glassy circlet of thorns weeping slow red tears down its forehead. "Welcome home, my son," The Father of All Colors whispered, its voice weighed down by infinite sadness as the dissolution set in.

The Sacred Dance...the miracle of life contained within human flesh. The Secret Life of Colors...

The Angel of Red twisted on the floor, struggling to shed Ashley's dead flesh. The girl's neck was broken and hung sickly. First with weak fingers, then gradually gaining strength, it opened the clotted muscle onto the cage of white bone beneath the flesh, and then like some grotesque butterfly the Angel began the screaming agony of its rebirth, coming out from the skin, breaking the cage bone by bone, taking Ashley off just as easily it had Lamenzo, but there was nowhere else to go this time when the Angel stepped out of the corpse. No body that hungered for life. It looked up, gasping for breath like some newborn, at the hole in the roof and the man who didn't want to live, at the rubble strewn about the church floor, the destruction marked by slabs of masonry and broken tile, and back at its own kind. It called out. It yearned. But there was no hate, no desire, strong enough for it to answer. No hunger for life for it to fulfill. It was over.

"I'm home," the Angel of Red breathed into the sanctuary of the church as the other colors silently made a place for him around the broken body. From its tongue, the words sounded like a curse. A sheen of blood clung with lover's intimacy to the Angel's true form, its wings of glass slowly unfurling from the wash of blood that matted them against its back.

GABRIEL Rush turned the music off and sank back into one of the worn–out loungers in Wind Runner's trailer. The bars of the electric fire glowed a steady orange, radiating heat.

He had tried but he hadn't been able to face the world with its questions and its need to know, to understand. How could he begin to explain the miracles of angels and serial killers to a sane, rational world so hungry to blame Bill Stern? The Trinity Killer? A cop gone bad, they whispered, killing his own. Driven to it. Driven to the edge. The Reservation had been a refuge, a place to hide. But it wasn't just that. Not if he was being honest with himself.

The legend of Worm Pipe clung to his feverish thoughts like a leech sucking the very lifeblood out of him.

Going into the Land of Dead Souls to bring a dead wife back...a dead son...a lover, the promise of a future...

"It isn't over," he whispered into the quiet room. With the music gone, the only sound in the room was that of the rain breaking on the trailer's roof. Christmas Day was twenty hours old. On the coffee table, photostats of the Trinity Killer's victims lay face up, so many dead, accusing eyes that wouldn't stop looking at him.

There was so much blood staining his hands, so many lives. He couldn't stop himself from thinking that he might have saved at least one of them if only he'd done something different, sooner...

Celine's blind eyes stared at the ceiling. She had her fake rose in her hand. The mark of the Trinity on her cheek. He'd drawn a red crayon 'Z' across her face: case closed. His own guilt kept him looking at the women rendered in memories and celluloid.

The television flickered blue ghosts about the trailer.

In one trembling hand, he held his old .38, in the other a silver bullet with his name on it. It would be so easy to just load the gun, open his mouth and pull the trigger. Exit stage left, Gabriel Rush.

And the sixty–four–thousand–dollar question, what would he be leaving behind?

"I'll take hopeless losers, for two hundred, Alex." Gabriel said to the television, playing Jeopardy with himself. "Mirror, mirror on the wall, who's the loser on his own? Tick tock... Tick tock...I know, that'd be me, Alex."

Nothing was the answer. Nothing at all. He'd moved on. The Reservation wasn't home, for all its beauty and all of the memories he associated with it, it was just another place where people didn't know him from Adam. He'd cried the tears, nursed the hangovers and watched everyone swallow the lies of real life. Was there a chance? Could he find a way across the veil to bring his life back out of the Ghost Lodge? He wanted to scream. Wanted to put the gun between his lips and just do it, pull the fucking trigger and end it all. Sink into the black where that ghost of hope would stop taunting him.

But there it was:

In death maybe, just maybe, they could be together.

It was stupid, but he couldn't help thinking that if there was a chance, even the slightest chance, that the stories Wind Runner told were true, he'd risk it. He'd tear down the walls between life and death from the inside out or the outside in to bring her back...

Gabriel slipped the silver bullet into the breach and put the .38's muzzle into his mouth. His finger closed ever so slowly tighter around the slick trigger. Easing it down.

He closed his eyes.

Ashley's face was waiting for him as it always was when he closed his eyes, beautiful, the way he wanted to remember her, only to die again, the bullets from his gun stealing the beauty with their brutal steel kisses. Her blood was all over his hands. It might just as well have been his bullets that killed her.

"Will you never forgive me?" he whispered to his hands.

Never, my Little Indian, a hateful voice flittered in his mind.

He quested about inside his thoughts, seeking out the Angel's touch, but his mind was lonely. A single personality dwelling in the darkness. Only him. Gabriel. Haunting himself.

Gabriel closed his mouth around the cold steel of the .38's barrel, tasting the sour gun metal on the tip of his tongue, like blood. He wanted so desperately to pull the trigger but just couldn't. He wasn't strong enough; or weak enough.

No, he was going to live and try to learn to live with the impossible hope, to live with the yearning for a miracle...

There was time for all the miracles now, for the angels and the ghosts to come, for women alight with their own hate, for born–again child killers, for undead priests doing the resurrection shuffle, for restless souls to stand forever on street corners awaiting forgiveness for their mortal sins. For an inner–city Wonderland, a world of glass and color where angels didn't fear to tread...to cross into the Land Of Dead Souls, to look for a love he could bring home...

Time was all he had.

"Maybe tomorrow," Gabriel said, slipping the gun back into its holster. "Maybe tomorrow."

Outside, it stopped raining.

Welcome to the DarkTales Horror Community...

Check out the DarkTales Online Horror Community website at http://www.darktales.com. We are *the* haven for horror writers and artists on the web. Join our horror discussion list hosted by Onelist.com, put your website into our webring or submit it to us for award consideration, visit our bookstore to purchase your favorite horror titles, and submit your works to our editors for the various upcoming anthology titles and to our inhouse electronic zine-*Sinister Element*...

Sinister Element is the quarterly online publication of the DarkTales community. Insightful commentary on current events, the best in dark fiction, interviews with prominent figures in horror, and information you just can't get anywhere else—it's all here. *Sinister Element* also offers a unique opportunity for authors to get involved in the best collaborative fiction project that the horror genre has ever known: *Sawtooth Creek*. Under the Associate Editorship of Keith Herber, formerly of Chaosium Games, this is a once-in-a-lifetime experience for both readers and writers. Together with the upcoming *Best of Sinister Element* anthology, Darktales is providing opportunities no author or fiction fan should miss.

Visit *Sinister Element's* website at
http://sinisterelement.home.dhs.org

or visit the special Sawtooth Creek website at
http://sawtooth.home.dhs.org.

Join us...
We're Bringing Horror To The World!
www.darktales.com

The Asylum
Volume 1: The Psycho Ward
edited by Victor Heck

13 tales of madness by Douglas Clegg, Keith Herber, Sephera Giron, Scott Nicholson, Brett A. Savory, Steve Savile and others.

178 pages perfect bound $15.00

Demonesque
a novel by Steven Lee Climer

Rick Gilroy thought that getting out of big city police work prmised an easy future. Then a series gruesome murders shatter his plans for a quiet life in a placid town resort. When a beautiful psychic and an ex-occult insurance investigator get involved in the case, things only get more complicated.

166 pages perfect bound $18.99

In Memoriam:
Papa, Blake, and HPL
fiction by Mort Castle

Two stories from award-winning master author Mort Castle celebrating Hemingway, Robert Bloch, and H.P. Lovecraft. Includes The Old Man and the Dead *and* Teachers.

40 page chapbook $8.99

Scary Rednecks
and Other Inbred Horrors

stories by David Whitman
and Weston Ochse

Twenty-three stories of horror, madness, and humor set in the rural south. Includes Catfish Gods, The Great Appalachian Outhouse Feud, I Saw Renny Shooting Santa Claus *and twenty more.*

194 pages perfect bound $18.99

Order by mail or via the web at:
www.darktales.com

Secret Life of Colors was initially printed by DarkTales Publications in February, 2000, using Poppl-Pontifex type on 60# offset white. The cover is 10 pt. stock with glossy finish. The book was designed and typeset by Keith Herber. Editorial by Butch Miller. Proofing by Laura Elvin and Michael Moore.